WRATH'S
Embrace
TAWNY TAYLOR

ELLORA'S CAVE
ROMANTICA PUBLISHING

An Ellora's Cave Romantica Publication

www.ellorascave.com

Wrath's Embrace

ISBN 9781419961632
ALL RIGHTS RESERVED.
Wrath's Embrace Copyright © 2009 Tawny Taylor
Edited by Sue-Ellen Gower.
Cover art by Syneca.

This book printed in the U.S.A. by Jasmine-Jade Enterprises, LLC.

Electronic book publication May 2009
Trade paperback publication September 2010

The terms Romantica® and Quickies® are registered trademarks of Ellora's Cave Publishing.

WRATH'S EMBRACE

ဆ

Trademarks Acknowledgement

&

The author acknowledges the trademarked status and trademark owners of the following wordmarks mentioned in this work of fiction:

Cold Stone Germanchokolatekake Creation: Cold Stone Creamery

eBay: eBay, Inc.

Expedition: Ford Motor Company

Fox Reality Channel: Fox Entertainment Group

Home Depot: Home Depot, Inc.

Honda: American Honda Motor Company

Koenigsegg CCX: Koenigsegg Automotive AB

La-Z-Boy: La-Z-Boy Incorporated

Pepsi: PepsiCo Inc.

Popular Mechanics: Hearst Communications, Inc.

Saleen S7: Saleen, Inc.

Super Bowl: National Football League

Tiffany & Company: Tiffany & Company

Tupperware: Dart Industries Inc.

Prologue

ഌ

They are ancient. Masters of Sin. Fourteen men blessed by the goddess. And cursed.

During the Time of Darkness—the period mankind calls the Dark Ages—fourteen brave and honorable men willingly surrendered their souls to save humanity, accepting a portion of a spirit of sin within them so that humankind could finally break free from the shackles of evil.

With the dark spirits contained, the good spirits reigned.

Man was able to step out of the shadows at last—all men but the fourteen Masters of Sin, who struggle with the darkness every minute of every day, as they wait to receive their reward.

Chapter One

❧

Bruised, bloody and beat. That was when he felt best.

The voice was quiet. Blessedly silent. That was getting more and more rare recently.

Smelling worse than a hog bathed in sewage, Magus Lambard slid into the driver's seat of his Expedition, cranked the ignition and shoved his favorite CD into the player. Frowning, he glanced at the clock. At the peak of rush hour, among a horde of jerks who didn't know how to drive, was not the best time to be battling what would soon become overwhelming rage.

Dammit, why'd Coach have to keep them so late?

He pulled onto the street, punched the gas and breathed slowly as the pulse of the music echoed through his body.

Peace. Tranquility. Calm.

Nothing soothed better than Mehdi. Sweet melodies, performed on strings, piano, sitar and dulcimer. He hoped it would be enough to get him through this hell.

Damn it was hot.

Knowing how much the dark spirit loved the heat, Magus cranked the air conditioning full blast and concentrated on relaxing as he navigated through the maze of clogged freeways and congested streets that took him home. As he did every day, he swung by the ice arena to pick up Cyr Placett, his lover, best friend and the man who shared the other half of the spirit of Wrath.

And as Cyr did every day, he grimaced and smacked the power button on the radio, cutting off the music that had effectively lulled Wrath into a coma. "How can you stand to listen to this pussy shit?"

Instantly, Wrath roared to life, curling Magus' right hand into a fist. "It's soothing," he hissed, forcing his hand down to the gear shift instead of planting it in the center of Cyr's face like the spirit was goading him to do.

Shit.

As much as he loved Cyr — and he loved him greatly — the man knew exactly how to push his buttons. Both the right and wrong ones.

"Speaking of pussies," Magus growled between clenched teeth, "I think we both could use some of that right now — better that than I beat your ass."

Cyr threw his head back and laughed. "Beat my ass? In your dreams. The way you reek, the best you're getting is your hand or Hilde that idiotic sex doll Troi keeps stashed in his closet."

"I'm not touching that thing." Magus eased the Expedition into a lane next to the Honda that had been hogging all three lanes of the road for the past five miles, resisting Wrath's demand he flip the driver the bird when he was finally able to pass her. A toddler was screaming bloody hell in her backseat. He actually felt sorry for her. "Troi uses it."

"No shit?" Cyr poked the radio's power button, flipping to his favorite news station. "I thought he kept it in the closet, literally."

"He's possessed by the spirit of Lust," Magus said over a commercial for a mortgage company. Wrath decided the commercial was annoying enough to make a guy want to pound someone's face in. "What did you expect? There aren't enough women in town to keep him satisfied for more than a week."

"Still." Cyr shook his head as he leaned back. "How anyone can lust for a hunk of rubber is beyond me."

"Amun's worse."

"No way. Amun might have more than his share of Lust, but he wouldn't poke a rubber doll."

"Perhaps, but he'd poke a goat."

Their laughter kept the beast at bay for the rest of the drive, even when they were caught behind some jerkwad weaving between two lanes while driving twenty miles per hour below the limit.

Finally, after a hellacious drive, they pulled into the driveway, parking behind Amun and Troi's ridiculously overpriced cherry red Saleen S7 and Delius and Rane's even more expensive black Koenigsegg CCX.

Such a disgusting show of luxurious consumption, all four of them. Even so, they were outspent by another pair, who was driven by the spirit of Gluttony to spend amounts that made most men dizzy.

Both possessing Envy, Delius and Rane couldn't stand to be out-classed when it came to anything—clothes, cars and especially women. Which was why, to keep the peace, Magus had asked the masters of Gluttony to move out a long time ago.

Magus couldn't stand drama. Irritable by nature anyway, his portion of Wrath made him even more short tempered. Especially in the last couple of months.

Annoyed neither pair had bothered to park in the garage so Magus could pull what the other four called The Beater up to the house all six of them shared, Magus stomped on the brake and cut off the engine.

"I can't wait to move out of here," he said as he shoved open his door. "They're driving half-million-dollar cars. We could all afford something bigger, but still they insist we stay here, in this neighborhood."

"That's because it's quiet and the neighbors leave us alone. It won't be too long now." Cyr kicked the Saleen's front tire and the siren triggered, the annoying squeal grating

Magus' already frayed nerves. "Lucky for us the house next door'll be empty in a week or two."

"If we have to stay here, I guess it's the best we can do. We'll have our own space but still be close enough to keep an eye on each other and vice versa." Magus threw a glance over his shoulder, took one last glaring look at the twin sports cars then glowered at the cheery petunias planted in neat little rows along the front porch. "We'll have our own driveway. And our own gardener." He pushed open the front door, stepping into the foyer. "Wonder what the little brats have been up to today."

"Brats?" a male voice echoed from deeper inside the house, mocking laughter lifting the tone.

Everything was a laugh to the little bastard, Troi. Wrath itched to show Troi something truly funny.

Shoving the spirit's suggestion aside, Magus headed straight toward the stairs. A long shower would do wonders. Then maybe he'd pay a visit to his favorite submissive. Sweet little pain slut that she was, Jolie's willingness to please and high tolerance for pain made her the perfect partner for play. The games eased his burden for a short time. But only for a little while.

Never did the relief last long.

Not after a hard workout. Or even after taking a beating on the field during a game. Within an hour, the anger returned. Burning. Churning. Tying his insides into searing hot knots.

If only he could find relief that lasted longer. Two hours. A day. Oh what a wonder it would be not to feel this way for a whole day. Or two. Imagine a week.

But he'd long come to expect that would never happen, regardless of what the goddess had told them that dark day so long ago. She'd promised they wouldn't suffer forever. That someday their sacrifice would be rewarded.

Yeah, sure.

His glum thoughts for company, he headed into the bathroom to try to tame the beast where it was safe—away from everyone.

* * * * *

Something smelled bad. Not bad like a skunk having been mistaken for a cat. Or like a deadly cocktail of cleaning products having been mixed together. But like something burning.

Again.

Cursing under her breath, Gina Charis clutched at the towel wrapped around her body toga-style and raced down the hallway toward the kitchen. "Grandma!"

No answer.

"Grandma!" She waved the smoke away from her eyes. She'd forgotten to unplug the stove again. Dammit. Racing as fast as she could down the hall and through the living room, she smacked hips and shoulders into dainty tables littered with ceramic critters, and shelves loaded with candlesticks and Christmas figurines.

Around the corner she dashed, through a dining room housing a dining set that took up way too much room for her to navigate in a hurry, and that was without a gray cloud blinding her. Choking on smoke, she tripped, lurched and stumbled forward.

Finally, she made it into the kitchen in one piece, though slightly battered and bruised.

An angry blaze flared from a soup pot on the stove.

The guilty party was nowhere to be found.

Gina grabbed the fire extinguisher off the counter—it was always close at hand—and doused the flames. Once she was sure the fire was truly out for good, she padded barefoot through the house, calling for her grandmother.

Not in the family room, in her usual spot on the couch. But her grandmother's favorite television show still blared from the old set sitting in the corner.

Not in the basement.

Or garage.

Or in her bedroom.

She checked the front door. Unlocked.

Dammit. Not again!

Her search had taken her almost full circle, to the hallway. The bathroom and her bedroom were just around the corner, so Gina grabbed the first bit of clothes she could find, jumped into them — literally — and raced outside into the early evening.

Right. Left. No sign of Grandma.

She jogged around the perimeter of the house, shouting "Grandma!" at the top of her lungs.

No response.

She stood in the middle of the enormous backyard, looking between lilac shrubs ablaze in purple petals, toward the property line. Beyond the wooden fence was a corn field, thankfully only neck-high with corn. No Grandma. She turned left, searching the neighbor's backyard, which sloped down to a creek on the far side. No Grandma. Still, because her grandma tended to head that way when she got out, Gina jogged around the side of the neighbor's house, toward a pair of French doors.

She stopped.

Her grandmother was inside the neighbor's house, dressed in a getup that would get a girl arrested for indecent exposure. And she was surrounded by at least five men. She wore quite the naughty smile on her face.

"Oh Grandma. Some seductress you are."

Little did the sweet old lady realize that the whole vixen look she had going on was ruined by the pink plastic rollers in her wispy hair and sloppily applied makeup. Blue eye shadow smudged up to her eyebrows. Red lipstick smeared all around her mouth. Glaring pink rouge circles on her cheeks added to her clownish appearance. Still, she was batting nonexistent eyelashes, pursing lips and swaying hips like a twenty-year-old.

Gina had to smile.

The guys gathered around her grandmother were all grinning at her good-naturedly. One offered her a seat on the couch. Another brought her a glass of something. Grandma gave him a kiss on the cheek.

"You go, girl," Gina whispered, chuckling.

It was such a shame to spoil her grandma's fun. Yet, on the other hand, Gina had to make sure her vivacious little grandma — with a thing for younger men, it seemed — wouldn't wander off again.

Reluctantly, she knocked.

Six sets of eyes snapped to her.

Her grandma's smile widened.

One of the men stepped up to the door and opened it. He was huge, towering over her by at least one foot, maybe two. His arms were thick, shoulders impossibly wide. If he didn't play football for a living, he had missed his calling. "Hello." His voice was super deep. Uber sexy.

"Hi. Um. That's my grandma."

His gaze snagged hers for a split second, and something crossed over his features for the briefest moment. Then he stepped aside. "Come in."

"Oh there you are, Erma," her grandma said. "Why are you knocking on your own door, dear?"

"Erma?" the man at the door echoed.

"No, actually my name is Gina. I moved in with my grandmother a few weeks ago. She has Alzheimer's. They adjusted her medicine again, but I don't think it's right."

"Hmmm," he responded, moving closer.

14

A little shiver of awareness swept through her body. "Grandma, how about we head home now? I'm sure these men have other things to do."

Her grandmother pursed her lips. "I'm not leaving yet. The party just started."

"Grandma, please."

Her grandmother shook her head. "Why are you being so selfish? There are five of them, and look, there isn't an ugly one in the lot. I tell you what, you can have two and I'll have three..." Grandma reached for the guy closest to her, who had long silver-blond hair, a stunning face that invited a girl to stare, and a to-die-for body. "Troi's my first pick. Your turn."

The chosen, Troi, chuckled.

"Go ahead, Erma. Don't be a ninny. Pick," her grandmother goaded.

"You called me a ninny?"

A sexy rumble came from the guy behind her, the sound making her feel all warm and soft inside. It was most definitely a nice sensation, one she hadn't felt in way too long.

Shaking off the pleasant quivers, Gina rushed over to her grandmother, taking her hand to coax her out of her chair. "Grandma. That's not how it works."

Grandma smacked her hand away. "Fine. If you're not going to pick then I'll go again. I'll take him. Cyr." She pointed over Gina's shoulder and Gina twisted to give the scrumptious guy behind her an apologetic smile.

Cyr didn't look offended. Then again, she doubted he would be offended, since she guessed he hadn't heard her grandmother. His gaze was glued to her ass.

Ohmygod. Gina jerked upright.

In her haste to get dressed, she'd thrown on the old pair of shorts she'd kept from college. They were comfy for lounging around the house, and handy for cleaning, since she

15

didn't care if they got bleach splashed on them or grease smeared over them.

They were ugly. They were worn.

And they were short. Very short. Clearly, obscenely short, particularly when she was bent over.

She yanked on the back, and his gaze snapped to hers. Slowly, a smile pulled the corners of his mouth up, and her head got a little spinny. She threw her arms forward, bracing herself against the chair her grandmother was still stubbornly seated in.

Wow, was he intense.

Gorgeous.

Sexy.

It had been too long since she'd been touched by a man. Held by a man. Even looked at by a man.

Did she really need to rush out so quickly?

"Cyr, come on over here and rub my shoulders, will you? I've got a nice treat for later, if you're a good boy." Grandma waggled her eyebrows, and Gina's stomach did a little flip.

This was getting disturbing.

"Okay, that's enough." Gina took her grandmother's hand more firmly this time. "These men have...work to do now. To get ready for the party," she lied, giving Troi, her grandmother's first pick, a pleading glance. "We'll come back later when they're ready for us."

Grandma twisted to the right, "You mean the party hasn't started yet?"

Troi—thank God!—played along. He shook his head, a very believable expression of regret spreading over his face. "I'm sorry, sweetheart. The party doesn't start for several hours."

Gina mouthed "Thank you!" as she helped her grandmother to her feet. Slowly, she led Grandma toward the

French doors, thanking Cyr when he opened them for her once again. "We'll see you later, gentlemen. Thanks."

"Our pleasure," Cyr said, a haunted, wicked smile still on his face.

"Who? What?" another man said from the far end of the room.

What a voice. Smooth and rich as *crème brulee*. Gina had to turn to look. She just couldn't resist.

Mmmm. She was glad she hadn't.

He was every bit as big and muscular as Cyr, and equally stunning. His hair was a riot of damp, heavy waves that fell to the tops of his well-formed shoulders. He had piercing eyes, even at a distance, and the most amazing face. The perfect combination of hard, firm lines and interesting angles.

"This is Gina and you know Isobel," Cyr said.

"Oh yes, I know Magus," Grandma said saucily. "But this here isn't Gina. This is Erma, my friend. She lives in this...house? Wait a minute. What are you boys doing in Erma's house?"

"It's nice meeting you." Gina gently pulled her grandmother toward the open door. "I think I'd better get my grandma home. She's a little confused," she whispered to Cyr.

Cyr's gaze slid to one side for a split second before returning to her face. "It was nice meeting you too, Gina. Very nice."

A very unsettling energy buzzed between them for a split second. She cleared her throat and waved at the rest of the men, standing behind him. "Sorry for the intrusion."

Gina realized as she walked her grandmother back to her gray and white brick ranch what a strange, almost surreal moment that had been. There was something about that man, the one her grandmother had called Cyr. He was attractive. No doubt about it. But there was more. A connection she hadn't felt with a man in a long time. Same with that other one, Magus. How strange, that out of a room full of beautiful men, some more gorgeous than others, those two had stood out from the rest.

A part of her wished she might have the opportunity to explore what that connection meant. Another was relieved. The shadows she'd glimpsed in their eyes told her they weren't exactly the quiet, docile gentlemen they appeared.

Chapter Two

ॐ

Cyr couldn't help himself. He let out a whoop. Leapt into the air. Threw his arms around Magus and gave him a hearty hug.

"What the hell?" Magus pushed out of his exuberant embrace.

"Didn't you feel it, Magus? Goddess, it was the most amazing sensation. Sweet, pure inner peace. Glorious."

Amun's dark features pulled into a mask of confusion. He stepped forward. "What are you saying, Cyr?"

Cyr clapped his hands on Amun's shoulders and gave them a shake. "The blessing! It's come. She's come. And none too soon. You remember what the goddess said? Some day we would get our reward. A woman would silence the beast—"

"No." Magus shook his head. "Can't be. I didn't feel any differently. And I should have felt it before you. I have the larger portion of the spirit."

Cyr shrugged. "I don't know why it is then. But I know what I felt. Or rather, didn't feel. It was silent, Magus. I heard not a whisper. Unlike now, I felt nothing. Goddamn, it was good not feeling like I need to beat something to pieces before I burn up." Wrath growled within him as he met Magus' doubtful glare. "I was closer to her. That must be why. Let's go talk to her again. Get close this time. You'll feel it. I swear you will."

The spirit roared, *No.* Rage flared in Magus' eyes, and Cyr's gut clenched. Wrath was as pissed as a cat hurled into a pond, all sharp teeth and claws. Raking at Cyr's insides. Tearing. Hissing.

19

Cyr felt his fists clench. Jaws clamp. Blood burn. "Shit, it's mad."

"Dammit," Magus agreed, slumping forward. "Hasn't been this bad before." He staggered toward the French doors, kicked them open and charged outside.

In agony, Cyr followed, sprinting across the yard, legs carrying him as fast as they could go. Arms pumping. Heart slamming against his breastbone.

Such fury. Blind fury. Wrath was screaming inside his head, demanding he commit all sorts of heinous acts.

No! Nonono! Won't lose control.

He ran harder, desperate to release the pent-up energy somehow. He pushed himself to the verge of collapse. Still the monster's voice didn't quiet. Its grip on him didn't ease.

The woman.

He turned and ran back, toward the gray brick ranch next door.

"I'll make you shut the hell up," he yelled. "She's the one. That's why you're so fired up."

The monster's enraged roar sent him hurling to the ground. He scrabbled back onto his feet and ran harder, faster. He didn't care if the beast beat the shit out of him, he was going back to her. There might be hell to pay afterward, but already he knew it would be worth it.

The peace. Oh goddess, the peace.

Wrath fought his every step as he ran. It screamed threats. It beat at his insides until he felt like they'd been yanked from his body, run through a meat grinder and stuffed back in. Still, he forced himself to keep going. Through a field of chest-high corn. Over the fence. Across her yard. To her glass patio door.

Struggling to catch his breath, he stood with hands braced on his knees. Magus ran up to him, looking as beaten as he felt.

"What the hell's happening?" Magus snapped. "I want to rip something apart. It's been worse lately, but not like this."

"The beast doesn't like what she did."

"We shouldn't be here then."

"Yes. We should. We need her."

Magus gritted his teeth, punched an apple tree then shook his bloody hand. Skin broken. Bones protruding. The wound healed within seconds. "Hard to control..."

Cyr nodded. "Need her now." The rage gripped him so fiercely, he fell to his knees.

"What if she makes it worse?"

"Worse? Couldn't." Cyr slammed his fist against the glass door.

The beast growled when it didn't shatter.

The curtain parted, revealing the lit interior. And her face. Her smoky-gray eyes widened with surprise.

She didn't move for several seconds.

He didn't speak. Neither did Magus.

The beast's voice quieted.

The burning eased.

Sweet goddess. He could breathe. What glorious relief.

He turned, caught Magus by the elbow and hauled him to his side. "Can you feel it now?" he whispered

"Yeah." Magus lifted his head and beneath Cyr's hand, Magus' arm relaxed.

"Is something wrong?" Gina yelled through the glass.

"Yes," Cyr said.

"Yes?" she echoed, jerking backward.

Shit! "I mean, no," Cyr corrected, desperate now to have her closer. He ached to touch her, to feel her silky hair slide between his fingertips. To hold her in his arms.

So lovely. Perfect. Wonderful.

"Can we talk? For just a minute?" he asked. Damn, he sounded desperate. Almost as desperate as he felt.

Looking confused, she shook her head. "It's pretty late."

Her gaze hopped back and forth between his face and Magus'. Her brows furrowed, the motion creating the cutest wrinkle between them. "I don't know."

"It's about your grandmother," Magus offered.

"We rang the bell, but you didn't answer," Cyr added, figuring she was probably wondering why they'd pounded on her back door. Normal visitors would use the front.

"Oh yeah. We need to get that fixed." Her body visibly tensed for a moment then softened. She nodded. "I guess. But for just a minute. My grandma's sleeping, and I need to get some things done while she's out." She looked leery as she unlatched the door, and when they stepped inside, she moved back, placing herself on the opposite side of a La-Z-Boy recliner. She propped her elbows on the top. "What's up?"

Searching for something to say, anything that would keep him close to this wonderful woman for more than a few minutes, Cyr started, "We'd like to…"

"Offer to help with Isobel," Magus added.

Fucking brilliant!

"We see she's a bit of a handful." Cyr stepped closer to the chair.

One arched brow lifted. "Um. That's very nice."

"That is, unless you already have some help." Cyr glanced around the room, searching for any sign that a man was staying in the house with the two women. He wanted to believe the goddess wouldn't send them a woman who was married or engaged, but who knew what the goddess might do. "A husband or boyfriend…?" He plucked up a copy of *Handyman* magazine. Checked the date. It was two years old and the label was addressed to Isobel's late husband, who had died roughly two years ago.

"And if I said I do have a husband?"

He smiled at the laughter he heard in her voice and set the magazine back on the table. "I'd ask why you're lying." He crossed his arms over his chest while holding her gaze, defying her to deny the truth.

She lifted her chin, ever so slightly. "And what makes you qualified to care for my grandmother? Are you a nurse? Doctor?"

Ah, so she was intentionally avoiding the topic. Interesting.

"No, actually we're professional athletes," Magus responded.

Her eyes darkened. "I see."

"That doesn't mean we aren't able to keep her safe," Cyr offered, more determined than ever to find a way to pay regular visits to their lovely Gina. He wanted to spend every moment he could with her. And it wasn't just because she miraculously ended the torment within him. She intrigued him. Captivated him. Entranced him.

He glanced at Magus and sensed he was as bewitched too.

There could be no doubt. Gina was the one, chosen by the goddess. Their blessing. Their deliverance. Their hope.

"You can trust us," he said.

Trust them? Seriously?

Gina shook her head. "Where I come from, trusting a stranger can get a girl killed."

What were these men really doing here? She was dying to ask them, but she had a gut feeling they wouldn't tell her the truth anyway. Instead, she decided she'd let herself enjoy their game. This was the most fun she'd had with a member of the opposite sex since moving in with her grandma.

"I mean, I don't even know your names," she lied.

Magus stepped forward, offering a hand. "You're right. We weren't formally introduced. But we can take care of that right now. I'm Magus."

"Magus," she echoed, accepting his proffered hand and giving it a shake. He had large hands. Strong. And when his fingers curled around hers, a current of energy zipped up her arm. A mini-explosion erupted in her belly. It felt very good.

"Cyr." Cyr thrust his hand out, and she released Magus' to relish the sensation of another strong, large hand folding around hers. Like Magus, Cyr had a solid grip, and they both gave her hand a proper shake, rather than a limp, weak one. Also like with Magus, the simple touches produced aftershocks throughout her.

"Cyr," she repeated. Her gaze locked to his and the world seemed to fall away. He was the center of the universe for one, two, three amazing seconds.

Magus cleared his throat.

"Okay. Um..." She hated releasing Cyr's hand but she did so anyway, lifting her arm to press her fingertips to her cheek. Her face was blistering hot. Her insides were churning like a storm-tossed sea, which was, oddly, not an unpleasant sensation. "I know your names now. That's a start, I guess."

"Sure it is. And your grandmother knows us too. Very well." Cyr tucked a thumb into the front pocket of his jeans. The motion drew her gaze to his crotch, and she couldn't help noticing the bulge pressing at the front fly of his pants.

That was one very large lump, which meant...she hadn't been the only one feeling the chemistry. The burning on her cheeks amped up another zillion degrees or so.

Cyr continued, "Around here, things are very different. Neighbors help each other, Gina."

"Sure." *Quit staring at his crotch!* She yanked her gaze away, turning her attention to Magus instead. "I'm sure they are different. I mean, they do help each other."

Magus' lips curled up into a knowing smile.

Busted!

Sure she was about to melt, she jerked her attention back to Cyr again, this time focusing on the terrain north of his nipples.

He possessed an amazing face. Dark eyes. Straight, perfectly proportioned nose. Sharply hewn cheekbones and a mouth that was more tempting than a Cold Stone German-chokolatekake Creation. She had a feeling he would taste decadent. Delicious.

She caught herself fanning her face and shoved her hand down into the crevice behind chair's overstuffed headrest. Good grief, there was enough chemistry in the room to set off a nuclear blast.

Now that these two men were closer, in a more intimate setting without the distraction of all those other men, she couldn't help but feel slightly overcome by the electricity zinging and zapping around them. She also couldn't help noticing the way their eyes tracked her, their bodies responded to her every word and movement. Muscles thickening. Pupils dilating. Breath quickening.

She combed her fingers through her hair, nervously toying with a curled tendril, and they marked her every motion. She pressed her fingertips to her lips, and Cyr's jaw ticced. Magus' eyes darkened.

Those were two powerful, strong, hungry men.

Standing as she was, with them looking at her like that, she felt sexy, in control but also vulnerable at the same time. She didn't want this moment to end, this subtle game of cat and mouse. Temptation. Flirtation. Seduction. Yet, even though her body was ready to take things to the next level, her head was most definitely screaming dire warnings.

Both men let off a dangerous vibe. She didn't know if it was because of what they did for a living or some other reason. Playing any kind of sport professionally would probably make a man aggressive.

She liked aggressive, if it was directed along the right channels.

They were also probably possessive as well. Most aggressive men were.

She liked possessive too, again, if it was directed along the right channels.

And professional athletes were dangerous. Most definitely dangerous.

She even liked dangerous, as long as the man — or men — in question weren't violent or cruel. A criminally violent man, she could not, would not, tolerate. The kind of man who wanted her and let her know it, who demanded her obedience and submission in the bedroom, and who let her know in a subtle way that she was his and he hers when they were in public made her melt.

At this point, she wanted to believe both these men could be like that, but she feared the kind of danger that glimmered in those dark eyes was something far more sinister.

They couldn't expect her to trust them with her grandmother. They were strangers. With absolutely no qualifications to care for an elderly woman with serious health issues.

"I'd better get back to work." She stepped to the side, coming out from behind the chair. She was still wearing those uber-short shorts. After all, the last thing she'd expected was to have anyone pounding on her back door. "My grandmother doesn't usually sleep more than a couple of hours at a time." She motioned toward the kitchen. "And I have quite a mess to clean up."

"Did you have a fire?" Opposite from what she'd hoped, Cyr sauntered toward the scorched mess, rather than toward the door.

"Yes, Grandma decided to whip up something for dinner. Unfortunately, it wasn't food."

"I see." He reached into the black pot and plucked up a piece of burnt cloth. She recognized it as the remains of one of her bras. Of course, her grandma hadn't burned her own clothes, she'd torched Gina's most expensive dainties. He dropped it and surveyed the damage around the stove. "It looks like you need some pretty extensive repairs. The counter's burned. The stove. The upper cabinet above. And the backsplash is blistered."

She hurried into the kitchen. "Shoot. I haven't had a chance to get a good look yet. I was hoping most of it was on the surface and I could clean it up."

"No. It's worse than that. The counter's ruined." He ran a fingertip over the laminate surface. "It should be replaced. No pressure, but if you'd like some help, we are both pretty handy around the house."

Now that was an offer she was tempted to accept. Although the kitchen was certainly usable, even with that section of counter being damaged, it looked terrible. There was no way she could afford to pay someone to come in and install a new countertop or hang a new cupboard. Her grandmother had very little left in the bank and her social security checks barely covered the basics. And because Gina had been living pretty much paycheck to paycheck when she'd been on her own, she had nothing in the bank either. She was just getting her new eBay venture up and running and had invested hundreds of dollars in sewing equipment.

"We can pick up a stock countertop at the local Home Depot and put it in for you," Magus offered.

"We work cheap. How's dinner sound?" Cyr added.

She surveyed the damage then turned to Magus. "Well, I don't know."

Both looked so eager it made her slightly uncomfortable. But what other option did she have? She could live with the damage, but sooner or later she'd still have to fix it. Once her grandma died, the house was going up for sale and she was moving back to the city.

Magus inched closer, and Gina's body responded instantly. Little tingles buzzed through her center. "This could have been worse." He too ran a hand over the charred counter, and strangely, despite the serious subject of their conversation, her imagination drummed up images of that same hand stroking her skin. "There's a lot of damage to other parts of the countertop, like here. This burn looks older. Has this happened before?"

She stepped to the side, only to bump into Cyr. She turned toward him, her gaze slowly wandering up, up, up. "Yes. I try to unplug the stove but it's such a pain to pull it out to reach the outlet. Or to go down...stairs...and cut the circuit breaker..." Her gaze locked on his mouth, and yet again, her imagination ran wild. Images flashed through her head, of those lips brushing softly over her collarbone, her nipple, her stomach. "I-in the basement."

Magus moved closer still, his body gently crowding her from behind. "We can also wire the stove with a switch so that you can shut it off when you don't want Isobel to use it. That'll stop this from happening again."

Cyr cupped her chin. "We want you to be safe." His gaze dropped to her mouth.

Was he going to kiss her?

She held her breath. Nerves jangled. Skin puckered. Little frissons swept up and down her spine.

No. Don't kiss me. I don't need the complication right now.

No complications. No kisses. Complications and kisses are bad.

Correction, kisses are good. So very good.

Yet another ripple of anticipation swept through her body. She closed her eyes and leaned back slightly, shuddering when her back brushed against Magus.

This was crazy, welcoming this kind of attention from these two men. Insane. But ohmygod, it felt so amazingly right.

She wanted to throw her arms around Cyr's neck and smash her body against his. More than she wanted to take her next breath. But for some reason she couldn't move. She just stood frozen in place, eyes closed, not quite leaning against Magus' bulky body. Waiting. Anxious. Nearly delirious with need. Trembling and burning.

Magus grabbed her wrists, fingers curled tightly. He pulled them behind her back, and a red-hot erotic thrill charged through her body.

Could they know somehow?

Even without wearing all the trappings of a sexual submissive, did she give off some kind of vibe? If so, this was the first time anyone had sensed it or acted upon it outside of a dungeon.

"Gina." Cyr's sweet breath caressed her face, her cheeks, her lips.

Another shudder swept through her body. "Cyr?" she whispered, still unable to exhale.

They weren't in a dungeon. They weren't playing. And maybe that was why she was reacting so powerfully. This moment, this intense, almost excruciating moment, was more thrilling than even her most wonderful experience in a bondage dungeon.

It was so…real.

Heat pulsed to her pussy.

"We will keep you safe if you'll trust us." Magus gathered her wrists into one of his hands and slid the other one around her waist. He flattened it over her belly, fingers splayed over her bellybutton and the tattoo hidden beneath her shirt.

Somehow, she knew he wasn't talking about the kitchen anymore.

29

Chapter Three

ဢ

She was perfect. Their Gina. His Gina. Soft and submissive. And yet strong. The goddess had been more than kind to bring such a beautiful woman into their lives. A blessing. Their blessing.

Now that she was here, and he had touched her, Magus couldn't stand the thought of being away from her. Not for a minute, let alone an hour or a day. The fact that she subdued the beast within him was only part of the reason why he hungered for her so badly.

She was simply too delectable, standing like this, submitting to his will, letting him touch her, explore her, discover all the wonderful surprises her body held for him.

Her face was that of an angel's. Pretty, in a very sweet way. But her body was made for sin.

With every miniscule glance, she sent simmering blood pounding through his chest. With every tremble and sigh, she sent that heat churning harder, faster. Magus' hands burned with the need to explore every inch of her body. His lips and tongue with the need to taste her. His nose with the need to draw in that glorious scent, of woman's sweet arousal. Even now, when they'd barely touched her, that smell hung heavy in the air. Intoxicating. Addictive.

"Safe." Magus bent to nuzzle the crook of her neck, and she eased her head to the side to allow him access.

"Safe," she repeated, her small voice quavering slightly.

"Yes." He inhaled. Ah, heaven. She smelled so delectable, fresh and delicious like ripe berries dipped in honey.

Unable to stop himself, he pulled her tightly against him, releasing her hands so there wouldn't be anything between his body and hers. Her soft derriere, barely covered by that scrap of worn material, pillowed his lengthening cock.

His tongue darted out, flicking over her skin, welcoming the first taste. Delicious. He wanted more. He took more. More tastes. More flicks, nips. Sucks. Meanwhile, his hand slipped lower, down over her mound to the hot juncture of her thighs.

When Cyr groaned, the pounding heat in Magus' body flared. Nearly blind with need now, he caught the front of Cyr's clothing and yanked until Gina was trapped between them. He lifted his head, staring at Cyr's mouth, and pleaded, "Kiss me now."

Cyr obliged, slanting his mouth over Magus', tongue slipping inside. Magus' mouth filled with Cyr's decadent flavor, a taste he craved constantly. Magus moaned into their joined mouths and stroked his tongue along Cyr's, losing himself in the pleasure of the kiss, this wonderful moment.

For the first time in hundreds of years, there was no anger. No rage to taint the pleasure. Only need. Desire. Profound wanting.

Between them, Gina whimpered.

He rubbed her pussy through her damp shorts and rocked his hips back and forth, desperate to grind away the ache pounding down the length of his cock. If only he could strip away her clothes right now and sink into her slick depth. He knew it would be incredible. Better than it had ever been.

Soon, he told himself. Not yet. The wait would be worth every second of agony he had endured over the centuries.

"I need you," Cyr murmured, echoing Magus' need.

"Me too. But I don't want to leave," Magus answered.

"Gina?" a female voice called from somewhere close by.

"Ohmygod, Grandma!" Gina stiffened against him, and he instantly jerked backward, twisting to glance over his shoulder.

Isobel stood with her hands cupped over her mouth, eyes wide. "I can't believe this. In my own house!"

Gina scurried to her grandmother. "Come on, Grandma, sit down."

Isobel shook a scolding finger at her. "I told you to share. And this is what you do? I picked Cyr first. He's mine."

Blushing sweetly, Gina steered her grandmother toward a chair. "Sit here. I'll get your tea."

Isobel winked at Magus. "After what I've seen, I need something a lot more potent than tea. And maybe a cold shower too."

Gina's laughter-filled eyes met his. She turned around, heading back to the kitchen, giving him a view of that tasty ass of hers, barely covered by those shorts. "You can't have anything more potent."

"You ruin all my fun," Isobel grumbled. She motioned to Cyr. "How about you two do some more of that kissing? What a show! I could watch that all night."

Gina's lips quirked as she said over her shoulder, "No, no. They have to leave now." She handed her grandmother a teacup.

Frowning, Isobel set it on the side table next to her. "Now that's not right. You got to be the meat in a manly sandwich. It's my turn." Isobel started to stand, but Gina kept her from getting up with gentle hands on Isobel's shoulders.

"It's okay, Isobel," Magus said, barely containing his laughter. Such freedom! Happiness. Simple, pure joy. "We'll be back tomorrow."

Gina gave him a confused look.

Isobel gave him an extremely pleased one. "Is that so?"

"We're going to be working on your kitchen," he explained. "You have some fire damage."

Isobel's smile broadened, and he wondered for a second or two if she'd started that fire intentionally. "Very good. You'll be here first thing?"

"After work," Cyr said, slowly heading toward the door.

"Excellent. I'll cook something special, assuming that granddaughter of mine will plug the stove in. She's so mean, doesn't let me do anything anymore. I'm a prisoner in my own home."

"We'll see, Grandma." Heading for the door, Gina gave them both a sheepish smile. "Good night, Magus. Cyr." She opened the door, holding it for Cyr. Something flashed in her eyes when he moved closer. Wanting. Even from a distance, Magus could see it plainly. When it was his turn to walk past her, he extended an arm slightly, letting his fingertips graze across her thighs. She audibly inhaled.

He stepped through the door. Walked about three feet from the house. And crumpled to the ground, cold, hard fury gripping him so fiercely he couldn't breathe.

How could he endure even a minute without her?

* * * * *

Delicious scents of roasting meat and baking pies filled the house.

This was how Gina remembered this place.

"Why won't you let me help?" Sitting at the small dinette table in the kitchen, her grandmother scowled.

"You did. You peeled the carrots. That was a big help." Gina lifted the lid on the crock pot and poked a fork into the meat to see if it was done. "There's nothing left to do." She replaced the lid and headed into the dining room to see if she'd forgotten anything when she'd set the table. Everything looked good. She headed back into the kitchen.

Her grandmother had once been such a wonderful cook, whipping up the most scrumptious meals every day. Meals that took a solid hour to consume, with appetizers, salads, meats, side dishes, home-baked rolls dripping with butter, and of course, dessert. Yes, her grandmother had a lot to do with Gina's love for food — as well as her ample hips and thighs.

Now it was Gina's turn to do the cooking, and she was sad to say she would never learn her grandmother's recipes. Grandma hadn't written a single one down, and all memories of them were long lost, thanks to the disease that was slowly stealing pieces of Isobel's mind.

Instead, Gina relied on prepared foods and pre-packaged meals most nights. But not tonight. She'd done her best to make something as close to homemade as she could. And she was damn proud of herself.

Roast beef, slow cooked in a crock pot, with lots of garlic and potatoes and carrots and onions. Tossed salad. Oven-warmed rolls with loads of butter. And a frozen apple pie, which she'd put in the oven a few minutes ago. It was already smelling scrumptious.

Between preparing dinner and sewing the first garments she would list on eBay this upcoming week, she had been too busy to be nervous, but now that everything was done — food prepared, house tidied, table set — all she could do was fiddle and fuss to try to burn off a little of the jittery energy zapping through her body.

She plopped down across from her grandmother and started pulling apart the paper napkin sitting in front of her.

"I think you need some tea," her grandma said. "Let's have a cup and talk."

Gina checked the clock for the umpteenth time. "Not now. They'll be here in a few minutes."

Her grandma tsked. "You're jumpier than a long-tailed cat in a room fulla rocking chairs."

"Am not."

Isobel lifted one eyebrow. "You can't lie to me. I've known you since you were in diapers. Why are you so nervous, dear?"

"Okay, maybe I'm a little tense."

Last night had been incredible. So magical, she'd dreamed of Magus and Cyr all night long. They'd starred in one pornographic dream after another. Touching, kissing, stroking and fucking her. Then they'd done the same with each other. She woke up with a tingle between her legs and a smile on her face.

But now all the tingles were different. Anticipation was making her jumpy, which was strange. This wasn't a date. And she wasn't so inexperienced or uncomfortable around men that she would normally get nervous. But these men were different than the average guy, and she found herself reacting to them in such a profound way.

Ironic, she'd spent years searching for a man who could make her feel like this, and now—when she couldn't let herself get too close—here he was. And there was more than one.

Two amazing men.

Two amazing faces.

Two amazing bodies.

Two.

After a long stretch of uncomfortable silence, during which Gina suffered terribly under her grandma's probing stare, she finally started, "It's hard to explain—"

Someone knocked on the front door.

"I'll get it." She scampered toward the door, taking deep breaths as she walked, hoping the guys wouldn't sense how anxious she was. She hadn't been this nervous on her very first date, for christssakes!

The visitor knocked a second time, just as she reached for the knob. She gulped one last deep breath, rolled her head from side to side to de-kink the muscles in her neck then opened the door.

Her insides lurched when she saw them. "Hi there." She pushed the screen door open to let them in.

Magus' dark eyes met hers. His lips curled up. "Hello, Gina." He stepped through the doorway, and just like that, her blood was simmering.

Behind him, Cyr gave her a smile as he too entered. In each hand, he held a black toolbox. Both were wearing work clothes—snug jeans and t-shirts that hugged their upper bodies like cheap whores. "Thanks," he said as he passed her.

"Um, dinner's ready." Still standing at the door, she admired the view from behind.

Those were two of the finest asses she'd ever seen.

While she shut the door, they moved out of sight, turning the corner toward the family room. She smiled at the sound of her grandmother's voice as she greeted their guests.

What a flirt. It was sweetly ironic that her grandmother's disease was giving her a glimpse of her grandmother's personality as a young woman.

Isobel was indeed quite the seductress.

When Gina turned the corner, she found her grandmother clinging to Magus. This time, her grandmother was dressed in her best outfit, hair fixed, makeup applied. Gina had even painted her fingernails for her. Magus was grinning, though his expression was tense, his cheeks ruddy.

Gina swallowed a chuckle. "Grandma, how about we eat? Dinner's getting cold."

"Yes, yes. I'm starving." Snatching Magus' hand, she headed toward the dining room, leaving him with no choice but to follow.

Gina grabbed the bowl of carrots and potatoes but before she got more than a couple of steps, Cyr gently took the bowl from her. A platter of meat in her hands, she followed him into the dining room, where she found her grandmother had positioned herself between the two men and had moved their chairs closer to hers.

"Now this is cozy," Isobel said, looking enormously pleased. "It's been such a long time since we've entertained. My granddaughter isn't much of a hostess."

Both men sent Gina questioning glances.

"I've just recently settled in," she explained, her cheeks warming. "And I'm trying to launch a new business." She offered the basket of rolls to Cyr. "I haven't had any time to get to know anyone."

"Thank you." He plucked a roll from the basket. "You know us now."

Not hardly. "Yes," she said, her eyes locking with his. He had this way of studying her. So intensely. Like he was trying to delve deep into her mind, search out her secrets. Still, as much as she wanted to look away and protect herself, she couldn't.

"I'd like a roll please," her grandmother said.

Finally, she turned her attention to her grandmother, who was holding one hand out patiently and waiting for the basket. "Sure. Here you go." Gina handed it over then helped herself to some vegetables and meat.

While she ate, she watched her grandmother flirt with the two men. They played along. Every now and then one of them would give her a meaningful look but they concentrated most of their attention on the elderly lady, and she enjoyed every minute of their smiles and generous compliments. Gina guessed her grandmother was having the time of her life, and she was content to watch quietly, allowing her grandmother to have her moment. There was no saying how many more moments like this she might enjoy.

After dessert, her grandmother bid her *boys* good night and retired to her room, leaving Gina alone with them.

They politely helped her clear the table. Each time they passed her, as they all carted dirty dishes and bowls of food to the kitchen then returned to the dining room for more, they gave her a look and a bright smile.

Then Cyr trapped her in the narrow doorway between the kitchen and dining room, stepping through at exactly the same time as she did. His bulk took up most of the space, leaving her barely enough room to wiggle past him.

"Excuse me," he said. "Gina."

Her gaze snapped to his. The air in the room instantly thinned, and suddenly her heart started pounding against her breastbone. He didn't move, just stood there being all big and hard and manly, making her feel small and vulnerable and sexy.

Somehow she made herself move through the door. But as she hurried toward the dining table for the third time, her back tingled and nerves twitched. Magus was standing on the opposite side, stacking the last few plates on top of each other.

Nothing left to take back to the kitchen.

She spun around, deciding she needed to head back into the kitchen anyway. Once again, Cyr stood in the doorway, this time looking like he was deliberately waiting there for her. He tracked her every movement with those dark, sharp eyes of his. It was an odd feeling, one she had experienced before but never quite like this.

Like when she went to the bar. She always sensed when a man was watching her. She could feel it. But with these two men, that feeling was a lot more intense. Instead of a warm tingly sensation tickling her skin, it took the form of a pulsing heat deep inside her body. It was hard to think clearly or function normally with so much going on inside.

She loved flirting. Adored playing a good game of chase with an aggressive man. Thus, her instincts were driving her to play along, give as good as she was getting. But then she remembered all the trouble that kind of game had caused in the past.

That cooled things off, pronto.

Sobered, she reminded herself of her responsibility to her grandmother and how impractical, not to mention stupid, it was to get involved in any kind of relationship right now, even a casual one. She had no privacy. No free time. And before she'd stepped foot in her grandmother's home, she'd vowed to commit her time and energy to the woman who had done so much for her over the years.

Wrong time.

Wrong place.

There was no way this could go anywhere.

Such a freaking shame.

No flirting back, she lectured herself. *You don't want to send these guys the wrong message.*

The wrong message, like they made her hot.

The wrong message, like they were guest-starring in her dreams.

The wrong message, like she wished Cyr would back her against the wall and kiss her to oblivion, like he had kissed Magus last night.

This time when she shimmied through the narrow space, she looked down at his feet. That did the trick. She got through without throwing herself at him like the shameless hussy she wanted to be. And once in the kitchen, she had plenty to keep her busy.

"I guess we'll bring in the rest of the supplies and set up the saw so we'll be ready to cut the new counter once we get the old one out," Cyr said to her back.

She threw him a smile over her shoulder. "Okay. I'll just finish up in here."

Cleaning up after dinner and moving things out of the way so they could work kept her out of trouble. For a short time. Then they returned with their tools, ready to tackle the first part of the job—taking down the cabinet over the stove.

She knew how to operate a cordless drill, and she'd even tackled a few simple home improvement projects over the years, but this project was a lot more ambitious than anything she'd ever tried.

The life-student in her wanted to dig in and help.

The cautious part reminded her it was far more prudent to just stay out of the way and watch.

She went with prudence. Still, she quickly realized that even a safe choice could have its rewards.

Two beautiful men straining, bending, lifting, moving. And there she was, with a front-row seat. Oh yes, what a show it was.

Maybe she couldn't start anything with these two men right now, but did that mean she couldn't indulge in some serious staring?

Silently, she conjured up a loooong list of improvements and repairs that needed to be done, wondering if it was a bad thing to take advantage of two men who didn't seem to mind.

Chapter Four

ℛ

A couple of hours later and the guys had the new cupboards hung and the doors installed. Gina was on the couch, pretending to watch television. *Dancing with the Stars* couldn't compete with what was happening right there, in her grandma's kitchen, even with her fave pro dancing a seductive rumba, hips swaying, hands roaming all over his partner's firm body.

But now the guys were outside. There was a lot of thumping and rattling as they gathered their tools. They would be leaving soon.

She'd be alone again.

Alone and lonely.

She glanced down at the romance novel in her hands, a paranormal story about a woman and a pair of vampires. How she adored her smut. Grandma did too. But for the first time, she couldn't read without feeling like she'd been cheated in life, forced to live vicariously through books because she couldn't have the real thing.

Not that a real man or a real relationship would be anything like the novels, thus the reason why she was now a confirmed bachelorette. Still, she was young and independent, and lonely and normal, and she craved a man's touch. She ached to be held, caressed sweetly then fucked roughly. Just like in her books.

She sighed. She hadn't guessed it would be so hard.

The door to the attached garage opened and Cyr entered the room. His expression darkened when his gaze met hers. "Is something wrong?"

"No. Nothing."

"You look...upset." He walked around the side of the couch, stopping directly in front of her.

The man was remarkably perceptive. It kind of made her feel a little uncomfortable, as if she couldn't hide anything from him.

Before she could figure out what to say, Magus came in. The two guys exchanged a look then his brows furrowed. "What's up?"

"Gina was just about to tell me what's bothering her," Cyr said, sitting next to her. Despite the fact that there was a large portion of the sofa unoccupied, he sat very close to her. She enjoyed that but didn't. Just like she enjoyed the fact that he could read her so well but didn't.

"Something's wrong?" Magus studied her as he moved closer, taking a seat on the couch's arm.

"I'm not upset," she explained. "I was just thinking."

"About?"

"About my grandmother."

Cyr's expression softened slightly. "We can tell she's getting worse. She's always been a bit of a flirt, but now she's acting like a woman half her age."

"Yes she is." Gina was glad to see the conversation moving into safer territory, even if the new topic wasn't exactly a happy one.

Magus nodded, leaned over and flopped an arm around her shoulders. She liked how it felt having his strong arm resting on her shoulders. Comforting. Soothing. "It must be hard for you to take care of her by yourself."

"I'm doing the best I can."

Cyr set one hand on her knee. It wasn't an erotic touch, but just like Magus' it felt wonderful. "You could use some help."

She stared down at his hand, tapered fingers with neatly trimmed nails. So unlike what she might expect, given what he did for a living. "I'm looking into some services. Visiting nurses, hospice, that kind of thing. But I haven't gotten very far yet."

Magus squeezed her shoulders, giving them a soft shake. "We're here to help any way we can."

"That's very sweet. Thanks." She glanced at Magus, gave him a smile then turned to Cyr. Something very special was happening here, something she hadn't expected. These men weren't only objects of lust anymore but were already becoming her friends. The kind she might talk to, share with, laugh with. Cry with. "When I agreed to come here and stay, I had no idea how difficult it would be."

"Or how lonely?" Cyr offered.

Too damn perceptive.

She nodded. "Sometimes."

He gave her a playful grin. "We'd like to help with that."

She chuckled and her cheeks warmed. If that twinkle in his eye was any indication, she knew exactly how he planned to help with her little problem. "How gallant of you to ease my suffering."

Looking not at all ashamed, Cyr shrugged. "Hey, you're beautiful. Smart. And sweet. What guy wouldn't want to spend some time with you?"

"Plenty," she blurted. She regretted saying that word the moment it was past her lips.

"Idiots. All of them." Magus gave her shoulders another gentle squeeze. "We want to spend time with you. If you'd like us to. We could take you out for dinner, or to a movie. Or just a walk, talk. Whatever you want."

"That sounds wonderful, but right now my grandmother needs me. She deserves to be my focus. I owe her that. I'm sorry, my social life is going to have to take a backseat right now."

"I understand." Cyr cupped her cheek. "Isobel is very lucky to have you."

"Thanks." Her gaze locked with his for a moment. There was a connection between them, a moment when everything and everyone else in the world faded away and the air crackled with electricity. His thumb brushed over her bottom lip and her gaze dropped to his mouth.

His lips parted, as if he was about to say something, but then he tipped his head and leaned forward to kiss her.

Dizzy, she closed her eyes and dug her fingertips into the couch cushion.

The kiss was fleeting, a teasing, tormenting touch. Then he did it again and again. Butterfly kisses sprinkled over her lips. Tender and sweet. Sensual. With every touch, a little spark ignited inside her. Poof, poof, poof.

She ached to plead with him to deepen the kiss, to take her fully, possess her hard. But she didn't. Instead, she whimpered and put up a show of resistance while secretly enjoying his sweet torment.

She needed to stop him, before it was too late.

Behind her, she felt Magus move closer. His heat warmed her back. His fingers wound in her hair. He pulled and her head fell back, her mouth stolen from Cyr's to be claimed by Magus'.

His kiss wasn't soft or fleeting. It was the hard possession she'd been aching for. The kind that inspired her to drop to her knees in submission. To bend her will and relinquish control to her Master.

With one kiss, he claimed her.

With one kiss, she surrendered.

Grandma was safe for a little while. The latches on all three doors would keep her inside the house and out of danger.

These men knew enough to not expect more than Gina could give right now…right?

"It is so hard," Cyr's hands smoothed slowly up her blue-jean-covered thighs, "to resist."

She shared their frustration. "I know."

His hands stopped a few inches above her knees. "I want to touch you. Taste you. Watch you writhe in ecstasy."

She wanted the same. Especially when Magus' tongue swept into her mouth. It took. Tasted. Possessed. "Shouldn't."

"Just once." Cyr's hands moved higher, and her thighs tightened, her knees parting. A pulsing throb began in her core. Thrumming heat pounded between her legs. "Only one time. We won't expect more."

"Promise me," she practically begged.

"We promise."

That was it, there was absolutely no reason to stop this if it would only be one night. She knew where it was going, and she was mighty glad to let it play its course. No expectations. No pressure. It would be just sex. Fun sex. A welcome release. A welcome relief from the loneliness.

It was a struggle, but she managed to break the kiss long enough to mutter, "Let's go to my room." She accepted a hand up from Magus, and giddy, walked on wobbly legs around the house, checking latches on each door before finally heading into her room. She closed the door then stood there, back pressed against the smooth wood veneer, and looked at them. She wasn't scared. She wasn't regretting her decision. But she was a little nervous.

There'd been no rules to read, no discussion about limits or expectations.

Cyr, sitting on the bed, patted the mattress while Magus coaxed her deeper into the room with a smile. Dark flames flickered in both men's eyes. Burning hunger. She could see it, even from a distance.

She would soon know what it felt like to have those flames unleashed. To be engulfed in their heat. A jolt of tingles swept up her spine.

It struck her then, she couldn't remember the last time she'd had sex without being tied up first. There were no ropes, no swings, no benches or fetish gear. The trappings of her former lifestyle. The one she had left behind.

She could only guess that was exactly why she felt so lost and unsure. If she wasn't expected to drop to her knees, what should she do?

Magus seemed to read her confusion. He reached for her hand and pulled her toward him, cupped her chin in his free hand and forced it up until she met his gaze. "Are you afraid?"

"Oh no. Not at all. It's just…" Unsure whether she could admit the truth to him or not, she searched his eyes. To her, Magus was the harder, more stern of the two. Quieter. More emotionally shut off. He was the type of Master she would have sought out in her former life. He was the kind of man who made her feel small and powerless, sexy and feminine. Safe.

"Just what, Gina?" He bent lower, softly brushed his mouth over hers. "Tell me your secrets. I want to know everything."

His words, delivered on a husky voice, with his mouth not quite touching hers, made her shudder.

"It's been a very long time," she whispered.

"I see." He reached around to the back of her head, tangled his fingers in her hair and tugged gently, forcing her head back. He kissed a blazing trail along her jaw, down her neck.

She shivered, started to lift her arms, but someone caught her wrists just as she started to move them. Cyr? Yes, it had to be him. Strong hands held them down at her sides, against her outer thighs. So sexy.

Her nipples tingled. Her insides simmered.

Warm. Tight.

Magus had kissed his way down her neck by now and was nipping her collarbone, hands moving along her waist. He hooked his fingers under the hem of her top and pulled, easing it up higher, higher, over her breasts, up over her head. Cool air caressed her burning skin. More goose bumps prickled her stomach and chest. More shivers swept through her body.

So good. So right.

Her shorts were next, sliding down over her hips, over her bottom, down her thighs and then she was standing in her panties and bra, eyes closed, lost in the pleasure of having not one but two men touch her, stroke her, kiss her. She lost track of whose hands were whose. It didn't matter anymore. All she knew was the pleasure. A teasing stroke down the line of her spine. A tickling caress over her stomach. A harder possession of her breast through her bra.

Her nipples hardened, the peaks burning slightly as they pressed against the lace cups. Her back tightened when a wave of warmth pulsed up her spine then back down. Her hips rocked back and forth, the pulse of her need thrumming hard between her legs.

She kept her eyes closed, shutting herself into a familiar dark cocoon, as if she were wearing her blindfold. All around her erotic sounds blended into a symphony. The soft smack of a kiss, the even softer sound of skin gliding over skin. Sighs. Moans. Whimpers.

The minute snap of her bra coming unhooked.

The almost imperceptible sound of the garment sliding along her arms then the plop as it landed on the floor.

The scuff of lace down her legs.

Nude.

She sighed, reached blindly, and held onto a pair of hard, thickly muscled shoulders that were thankfully positioned in front of her at about mid-thigh level.

Two male groans of pleasure echoed in the room, and she swallowed a moan and a whimper.

She was absolutely burning up. From the tips of her toes to the ends of her hair. And every miniscule part in between. Neither of the guys had touched her yet where she burned the hottest. When would they? Please, would they?

Someone was kissing her stomach. Softly. Little teasing butterfly kisses. The other was behind her, hands slowly moving up her legs, to the backs of her knees, higher. Oh yes, the backs of her thighs.

Higher! Please.

They jumped to her bottom, kneaded the soft flesh, and she slumped forward, feet sliding apart, supporting her weight on outstretched arms. They trembled. Her knees too.

All she could think about was her pussy, so empty. Warmth pounding through her tissues to the rapid tempo of her heartbeat.

A mouth closed over her nipple and pulled sharply.

She couldn't stand it any longer. She dropped down to her knees and swallowed a yelp. The last thing she wanted to do was make noise and wake her grandmother now. It would be absolute agony not to finish what they'd started. Pure torture. In a very bad way.

Strong arms cradled her, one beneath her knees, one supporting her back. She opened her eyes as she was lifted, discovered Cyr was carrying her to the bed. The expression on his reddened face was tense, yet he moved easily, fluidly, as if she were weightless. When he placed her on the bed, she lay semi-reclined, supporting herself on bent elbows, and watched as both men undressed.

With every garment that was removed, more gorgeous, stunning man was revealed. Bodies sculpted with hard planes, deep cuts between powerful muscle. Thick arms. Strong shoulders. Flat abdomens. Thick, erect cocks, tips glistening already with pre-cum.

Her cheeks practically blistered at the thought of both those rods sliding into her, pussy and ass, filling her completely.

She'd been double-penetrated before—by toys. Dildos. Never by two men. She was more than ready to try it now. Right now. Within the next ten seconds, please.

The duo moved toward her like a pair of panthers prowling toward their quarry. The fire in their eyes was hypnotic. She couldn't stop staring into Magus'. It was as if he'd snared her soul and was holding it hostage.

They climbed onto the bed, moving in perfect unison, two glorious gods, on their hands and knees. Sigh and double-sigh. They ran their hands all over her body. Legs, arms, shoulders, stomach, breasts, face. Cyr kissed her until she was sure she'd pass out from the pleasure and then Magus took over and showed her how much more delight could be had from a kiss. His mouth was magic.

While Magus taught her the true art of kissing, Cyr tormented her breasts. Pinching, licking, nipping. Lips. Teeth. Tongue. Fingers. He used everything at his disposal to bring her nipples to painful erection.

She was in agony. Sweet torment. Trembling, dizzy, inflamed.

Then Magus moved lower, totally skipping over her stomach, and her torture increased a hundred-fold. He pulled her knees apart and displayed his oral talents on the most sensitive part of her body.

"Ohhhh," she heard herself say on a moan.

So good. So fucking good.

His tongue danced over her clit, the pressure and rhythm absolutely perfect. With every flick, a blade of intense heat shot up to her chest.

Unaccustomed to having her hands free, she found herself leaving them lying at her sides, arms pressed against her body. But as she became more and more lost in the bliss

Cyr and Magus were so kindly delivering to every...single...inch of her body, she found she didn't want to do that anymore. She wanted to explore their glorious physiques. To map the planes of their abdomens and the swell of their shoulders. The thickness of their arms.

What glorious freedom! To touch, stroke, caress, fondle. As she wished, when she wished. She opened her eyes, looked at Cyr, who gave her a desperate look.

"Can I taste you?" she whispered.

He nodded, kicked a leg over her head and bent over to put his thick rod to her mouth. She flicked her tongue over the tip, tasting man and precum. Delicious. She wanted more. Needed more. Almost as desperately as she needed her pussy to be full of thick cock.

She closed her fist around the base and opened her mouth.

As if he was trying to time it, Magus slowly worked two fingers into her pussy at the same time. She groaned around a mouthful of Cyr.

Cyr growled like the beast she suspected he would become shortly.

And Magus said, "You are so fucking sweet. I could eat you all day."

She could never endure such agony. She wasn't sure she could take another five minutes of this.

He added a third finger, stretching her, filling her.

Desperate to make the guys suffer like she was, she relaxed her throat and took Cyr all the way to the base. With her fingertips, she traced the line from his testicles to his anus. Around his hole then back up toward his balls. As she explored his most private places, he slowly pulled his cock from her throat then gradually worked it back down.

Ohmygod, finger fucked and mouth fucked.

She wanted to come, craved release so desperately she would have begged if she could have. Magus' tongue was now swirling round and round her aching clit, the motion sending one intense wave of pleasure through her body after another. His fingers were sliding in and out of her pussy, tips grazing the most sensitive part. And her mouth was full of Cyr's cock, her head now cradled in his hands as he gently fucked her.

"Oh yeah, I want you so bad. I'm going to fuck you every way I can. Until you can't move," he promised. Unexpectedly, he jerked out of her mouth, angled steeper until his penis was lying on her stomach, the heat warming her skin. "Your tits."

She pressed her breasts together, the soft flesh cushioning his cock as he dragged it back toward her stomach and then threw his hips forward.

Magus kindly gave her a moment's reprieve but only long enough to don a rubber, push her knees wider apart, lift her hips and drive his rod deep into her wet, clenching pussy.

"Oh yesyesyes!" she murmured, eyelids heavy as she watched Cyr's cock surge toward her face then retreat. Once again, they moved in unison, Magus fucking her pussy, Cyr fucking her breasts. Forward, back, in and out. Each stroke ignited more blazes inside her body. Each thrust threw her closer to release. Closer, yes, closer.

Magus reached down and fingered her clit as he fucked her. Harder, he thrust, harder and faster. Yes, that was how she liked it, how she needed it. Cyr grabbed her wrists and slammed them up over her head, pinning them to the mattress.

Powerless. At their mercy.

She was going to come.

"Please?" she begged. "Can I come?"

"Yes, Gina. Come for us," Magus replied.

A nuclear reaction exploded inside her body. Whoosh. Heat rushed out from her center, followed by tingling and a sensation so intense she felt it in her scalp. Then came the pulsing release. Her pussy spasmed around Magus' invading cock, his rough fucking drawing out her pleasure.

Cyr groaned and jerked away and within a heartbeat, she felt a spray of wet warmth over her breasts. Still in the midst of her orgasm, she smacked her hands over her chest, smearing his cum over her skin.

Hotter. Tighter.

Would she come again?

She felt the sensation again—a gathering tension, winding through her gut. Magus dug his fingers into the flesh of her legs and the pleasure-pain sent her soaring once more. Colors exploded behind her closed eyes. She was lost in the erotic delight, and Magus was there with her, a deep, rumbling roar signaling his release.

Amazing.

Beyond words.

Absolute contentment.

So worth the weeks of struggle, loneliness. Leaving her job, friends, life.

Perhaps she was being doubly rewarded for that small sacrifice? Not only given the chance to spend some time with her grandmother before she was gone, but also finding a pair of very special men?

Chapter Five

ဢ

The agony burned through Cyr's body the moment he stepped out of the bedroom. Overwhelming, burning, churning rage. Unsure what to do, he glanced over his shoulder. Should he return to Gina's side, to peace and contentment, or run himself to exhaustion as he had before?

Shit, this was getting harder and harder. It seemed the dark spirit inside him reacted sooner each time he moved away from Gina, the excruciating pain driving him to pull her into his arms and crush that lush body of hers tightly against his own.

Stumbling forward, he propelled himself toward the bed. Instantly, the spirit silenced. Peace. He sat on the edge of the bed. Inhaled slowly. Gina. His woman. Their woman. Their salvation.

He could smell the sweet fragrance of her skin. Lovely. A bare, smooth-skinned leg was bent at the knee. Her hair was a tumbling, glossy mass. He had to comb his fingers through the waves. Cool satin. So soft.

Goddess help him, but he didn't want to leave her again. Not now. Not ever. And not just because of the gift she gave him just by being near. He wanted to give her something in return. Something equally precious.

But what?

Magus, sleeping on her other side, stirred, lifted his head and squinted at the glowing red numbers on the alarm clock. He whispered, "Does that say five?"

"Yeah. It's a quarter after," Cyr responded, knowing exactly how Magus felt.

"Damn." Magus sat up and pushed to stand. Slowly he stomped his way over to the attached bathroom.

As if she sensed him leaving, Gina whimpered in her sleep, threw an arm onto the pillow, where Magus' head had just been. Cyr smoothed his hand down her back and shushed her, and she responded instantly, stilling, the corners of her mouth pulling into a soft smile.

Stunning. What a beautiful, precious moment.

Cyr's heart felt like it was swelling, like all the ice that the dark spirit had caged it within had melted away, and he was happy. So unbelievably happy.

Ten seconds after he'd left, Magus rushed back into the room, eyes wide and face pale, arms wrapped around himself. "Shit, it's worse than ever."

Forcing himself to stand, Cyr nodded. "I thought it was bad before, but now...I went out into the hallway, and the beast was tearing me apart. Right outside the room. Ten feet away."

Magus slumped against the wall. "We can't stay here all day, every day. Forever. We have to go to work."

"Yeah, I know. But the fucking beast is howling so loud, tearing me up so bad, I'm going to need to be transported in restraints to keep from hurting someone."

"Our coaches'll love us."

"If we can get onto the field or ice without doing something illegal."

They swapped troubled looks.

"What if we took her with us?" Magus offered. "At least until we got to work. Then we'd be okay."

"What about Isobel? She won't leave her grandmother alone."

"She can come too."

Cyr shook his head. "We can't ask her to drag Isobel around twice a day. Somehow, we've got to control it. We've managed until now."

A soft rustle had them both turning toward the bed.

Gina was sitting up, eyes bleary, hair a tangled mass hanging around her shoulders. It took every bit of Cyr's willpower to keep from diving into that bed and dragging her against him again. She focused on Cyr. "What's wrong?"

"Nothing's wrong." He bent, allowing himself the pleasure of one small kiss. "We'll be back tonight to work on the kitchen."

She gazed up at him with a sweet expression on her face. "Actually, today's my grandmother's birthday, and I was thinking of taking her out somewhere special. Would you..." she hesitated, eyebrows drawing close, "both like to come with us?"

"We'd love to," they both snapped in unison.

Anything to be near their Gina.

She laughed. "Don't you want to know where we're going?"

"Doesn't matter," Magus said.

"Because we both love Isobel," Cyr added, hoping they didn't sound too desperate. To his ears, they did. Pathetically so.

He didn't like wanting her as much as he did.

When it came to women, he'd always been in control. Lust was acceptable. Expected. Wanting was okay too. But this was more intense than even wanting. It was...needing? He'd never needed a woman before.

A look. A touch. Just one. Then another. He craved them, like an addict did his next high.

Smiling at both of them, she gathered the sheet around her shoulders. He hated having that soft skin hidden from view. "Okay then. That's good. Because I'm not sure yet where

I want to take her. Maybe dinner. Can you be here at around seven?"

Cyr shook his head. "Shouldn't be a problem. Practice ends at four."

"Terrific."

Cyr gave her hand a final squeeze then watched as her slender fingers slipped from his grasp. "We'll see you later."

"Okay."

Out he stepped, into the hallway.

Into agony.

Into hell.

* * * * *

"I want to go dancing." Her grandmother crossed her arms over her chest and pursed her lips. "And not at one of those places where you young people gyrate against each other like a bunch of wild animals in heat. I want to go where people really *dance*, like I used to with your grandpa."

"Dancing?" Sitting at the kitchen table, the remains of her lunch sitting off to one side, Gina flipped open the phone book, turning to the d's. "Are you sure? I was thinking a nice dinner —"

"Bah. We have food here. Why would I want to go sit in some restaurant? That's boring."

"Okay. Dancing." Finding the heading *Dance*, she skimmed the page. Nothing looked promising, just columns of dance schools.

"I want to waltz. And rumba. And samba."

"Ballroom? Where does one go ballroom dancing?" Maybe she could buy her grandmother a lesson. Yes, that would be great. Maybe she could try it too. Oh, and Magus and Cyr could be their partners. It would be worth every penny to see those two stomping and stumbling around the dance floor.

An hour later, she had all the arrangements made.

The rest of the day, she spent helping her grandmother doll herself up for her big night. Hair washed, set and pulled into a romantic, curly up-do — a hair piece of silver curls taking at least fifteen years off her age — makeup applied, fingernails polished and best clothes donned, Isobel was primped and ready to go by six. While she ate a quick meal, Gina took a shower and hurried through her routine. It was fun, actually having somewhere to go, a reason to do her hair, apply some makeup and put on some nice clothes. When she'd been living on her own, she'd gone through this routine every day, never realizing how much she was taking it for granted.

This slower life had taught her some very interesting things about herself.

She was just applying her lipstick when she heard the guys knocking on the front door.

Isobel shouted from the living room, "I'd get it but you bolted the damn door!"

Chuckling at her grandma's bluntness, Gina dropped her lipstick into her purse and headed toward the living room. Isobel was glaring up at the bolt, positioned at the top. "Don't even think about trying it," Gina warned her.

"It's frustrating being locked in my own house."

"I know, Grandma." She rubbed her grandmother's shoulder then reached on tiptoes to unlatch the lock. With a twist of the wrist and a tug, she had the door opened, and there they were, two stunning males.

They looked amazing. Though there was something about their expressions that made them look stressed. A tightness.

"Hello." She pulled her cape over her bare shoulders. "I hope you aren't hungry, because Grandma doesn't want to eat."

"We're fine." Magus offered a hand to Gina, helping her down the step to the porch.

Cyr reached behind her to help Isobel. "You ladies look stunning. We are the luckiest guys on the planet."

Gina couldn't help throwing him a smile over her shoulder.

"Such a charmer you are." Isobel patted his cheek. "I hope you boys have your dancing shoes on."

"Dancing?" Magus led Gina toward the black Expedition parked in the driveway.

"It's what Grandma wanted to do. I found a ballroom dance school that has open nights, when visitors can come and dance with students and instructors. It'll be kind of like a party."

"Sounds nice," Cyr said behind her.

He didn't sound too thrilled.

Magus didn't look too thrilled either.

Not surprising. She'd yet to meet a man who loved dancing as much as she did. But this wasn't her fault. She'd warned them their plans were up in the air, but they hadn't cared this morning. They were all too eager to accept her invitation, no questions asked.

That'll teach them.

She couldn't help grinning as they drove to the studio, which was tucked into the back of a mostly empty strip mall. Curtains were drawn over the front wall of windows, but the light from inside cast shadows of the couples on the curtains as they twirled and glided around the room. The distant sound of a waltz echoed from the building.

Isobel clapped her hands. "Let's get inside. I can't wait to show these youngsters how it's done." She looped an arm around Magus' elbow. "Come on, quit looking so scared. I promise it won't hurt a bit."

His laughter was a low rumble.

Gina couldn't remember ever being so excited about a night out. Weird, since she'd gone to some great clubs with her friends back in her living-in-the-fast-lane days.

She followed her grandmother into the dance studio, with Cyr at her side. He cupped her elbow as she stepped through the door. Such a gentleman, so different from what she'd expected from a professional athlete. Every jock she'd ever known was an egotistical ass. Bossy. Possessive. Emotionally retarded.

Inside, Isobel headed for the front counter and announced, "Isobel Engel, we're here for our lesson."

The woman at the counter smiled, eyes sweeping over their group before catching Gina waving. "Go right ahead. First door on the left."

When her grandmother had moved away, Gina stepped up, purse in hand, and reached for her wallet. "How much do I owe you?"

"It's twenty-five dollars each."

Steep price. But it would be worth every cent if her grandmother had a good time. Silently, she thanked the Big Guy upstairs for her first eBay sale. "All right."

"I'll take care of it." Before she had the money pulled out, Cyr handed the woman a stack of twenties.

The woman quickly counted the money then said, "Thank you. Enjoy yourselves."

Gina turned to Cyr. "You didn't have to do that."

He folded his wallet and pushed it into his pocket. "No problem. Anything for Isobel." He motioned toward the doorway. "Shall we?"

They stepped into a huge room with wooden floors. One long wall was lined with mirrors, the reflections of dozens of dancing couples giving the illusion that the space was twice as big and filled with twice as many people. The music was loud but not enough to completely drown out the din of conversation, the scuff of shoes, the clack of heels.

She wound her way around the perimeter and stopped beside her grandmother, who was grinning like a child let loose in a toy store.

"What do you think, Grandma?"

"It's perfect. Thank you." She cupped Gina's cheeks and gave her a kiss then grabbed Magus' hand. The music changed, the rhythm slowing, tone darkening. "Oh goody, a rumba. Come on, young man. Let's see what you've got."

Gina watched her grandmother lead a reluctant Magus out onto the middle of the dance floor. Isobel threw one hand on his shoulder, extended the other arm and then rolled her hips like the young twenty-something girl standing next to her. "Look at her. Why does it not surprise me that she can still move like that?"

"Mmmm." Cyr's hand was suddenly at her waist and she silently let him steer her onto the floor. When he stopped, she turned to face him.

"I have no idea what to do."

"I'll show you," Cyr whispered as he pulled her closer.

"You know?"

His smile was positively wicked. "Surprised?" His hands dropped to her hips. Gently, he coaxed her to move them. "It's all about trust. Can you trust me?"

"Sure."

"Good. Now bend your knees slightly and transfer your weight."

Staring down, she concentrated on the motion, letting him guide her body. "Like this?"

"Yes, exactly like that. Very good."

A little quiver of pleasure pulsed through her body. Those words, the husky tone of his voice, both were heavy with sensual promise. Like Cyr wasn't just talking about a dance step but something so much more intimate.

She tipped her head back and looked into his eyes.

Dark desire.

There went another quiver. This dancing thing was beyond sexy. The music was sultry, slow, with a heavy beat. Their bodies swayed together in unison, a primal communication that went beyond words, beyond thoughts. A sway to the right then the left. A turn. He eased her away then pulled her close again, his hand flattening against her back, fitting her body snuggly against his. Again, she looked up into his eyes and she was instantly lost in the fire flickering in their depths, which seemed to flare with every thump of the music.

The bass thrummed through her body, carrying heat up through her chest, down to her pussy. It was as if the music was part of her. No, more like she was part of something bigger, more powerful. An ancient energy. Created by the joining of her body with his and amplified by the music.

It was magical, took her breath away.

But too soon the music stopped, and although the energy was still there, it eased. He stopped moving. She clung to him, feeling unsteady, legs a little wobbly and head a smidge swimmy.

"Are you okay?" he asked, supporting her with strong arms.

She was aware of every point of contact between their bodies. Where each of his fingertips touched her. His palms. His legs brushed against hers. Their torsos pressed together. "Fine. It's just...whew, that's quite a workout."

He gently steered her off the dance floor. "It is. Isobel has a bit of endurance for her age."

"Yes she does. I've seen it firsthand." Stopping next to the wall of windows, Gina turned to watch the dancers. She searched the couples, expecting to find Magus and her grandmother whirling to the music. A few seconds into her search, she located her grandmother. But she was dancing with another man. "Look at that, she out-danced Magus. But where'd he go?"

"He's over on the other side of the room." Cyr indicated the corner closest to the entry.

She looked in the direction he motioned.

As if he was suddenly aware of their gazes, Magus looked their way, smiled then started toward them. She watched him weave between people as he made his way around the perimeter of the room. As he walked, people glanced at him. Men and women. Old and young. Suddenly, she had no doubt why. He was a stunning man. But that wasn't the likely reason.

"Is that who I think it is?" she heard the woman closest to her say.

"Yeah. I'm pretty sure it is," came a male response. Then he said something else in a low voice. Gina couldn't make it out but she had a feeling she knew what he was saying.

How could she have forgotten? Magus and Cyr were both celebrities, professional athletes. One a professional football player. One a professional hockey player.

Gina didn't watch sports, which had made it easy to forget. But she was suddenly very aware of how many people in this crowded room knew who Magus and Cyr were.

A man stopped Magus before he'd rounded the corner and thrust a piece of paper at him. To his credit, Magus gave the fan a friendly smile as he signed his autograph. But before he'd handed the paper back, several more autograph-seekers had rushed toward him. Then more. More. Until he was fully surrounded by clamoring fans.

"Oh no." Gina swept the room with her gaze. "I hadn't anticipated that."

"Don't worry about it. We're both used to it. This is a small group. He'll sign a few dozen autographs and then it'll be over."

"I hope you're right." She motioned toward a man pointing their way. "It looks like you've been recognized too."

"Just stay with me." He pulled her closer, until her hip was pressed against his thigh. As a handful of people headed their way, he smiled, greeting them.

The next hour, Gina stood by his side, smiling but not speaking, listening to fans rant about missed shots or lost games, rave about lucky shots and won games. She smiled as fans posed next to Cyr for snapshots, even though she suspected she was positioned outside of the photographers' shots. Every now and then, she would try to step away, to check on her grandmother, but Cyr would catch her arm the instant she moved, limiting the distance she could travel.

Finally, the human wall around her thinned, the gaps allowing her to spy her grandmother dancing with the same man she had been earlier. She had a beaming smile on her face. Her cheeks were pink. Eyes sparkling with life and joy. Relieved, Gina felt herself smiling as well.

When the last fan left them, Magus approached, wrapped an arm around Gina's waist and gave her a little squeeze.

She looped an arm around his waist. "I'm sorry about that."

He smoothed a stray strand away from her eye. "No need to apologize. It's part of our job." He motioned toward her grandmother. "At least it hasn't ruined Isobel's evening."

Standing on Gina's other side, Cyr threw an arm over her shoulder. "Isobel looks like she's having the night of her life."

"Yes she does."

At that moment, the music ended, and her grinning grandmother waved. Then she turned to her partner, patted him on the shoulder and led him toward Gina and her two handsome escorts.

"This is my granddaughter, Gina," Isobel said as she stepped up to them. "Gina, this is Hank. He's an instructor here at the school."

Hank extended a hand. "It's nice to meet you. Your grandmother is a talented dancer."

"I see that now. I had no idea," Gina admitted, smiling at the kind-looking, white-haired gentleman who she guessed was in the same ballpark age-wise as her grandmother. Astonishing that a man at his age could have the endurance to make it through even one dance, let alone teach for who knew how many hours. "I'm afraid I don't share my grandmother's talent."

"That's not true." Cyr gave her shoulder a little shake. "You're a natural. You just don't have the training."

Hank lifted a brow. "We're offering a discount for new students, if you're interested."

"Oh I don't know."

Her grandmother scowled. "Of course she'll take lessons. I insist. We both will."

"Excellent." Hank glanced at Cyr. "We could always use more gentlemen."

Cyr nodded. "Sure, I'm interested."

Hank's gaze swept over to Magus.

Magus grimaced. "Oh I don't know. Isobel danced circles around me. I don't think this is my thing."

Gina understood how Magus felt, so she wasn't about to try to convince him to change his mind.

Her grandmother, however, wasn't so kind. "Oh now. It'll be good for you. Look at Hank here. He's in better shape than you young men, and he's more than twice your age. I insist you try at least a few lessons."

Magus gave Isobel a kind smile. "I guess that settles it then."

"Good." She patted Hank's hand then winked. "We'll see you soon. I should get these kids home now."

Hank beamed back. "I'm looking forward to it, Isobel."

Gina felt a smile spreading over her face. What was this? Was she witnessing a new romance blossoming? Between her grandmother and the dance teacher. How adorable was that?

Her grandma didn't say a word, just started shuffling toward the door, leaving Gina, Magus and Cyr to follow, exchanging knowing grins. Gina sat in the backseat next to Magus on the drive home. Cyr drove, with her grandmother in the front passenger seat.

The excited elderly woman chattered nonstop about the dance competitions she'd attended so many years ago. The ones she'd won. As well as those she hadn't. And the many partners she'd had through the years.

Gina had never heard these stories, had never seen any evidence of her grandmother's dance career. She enjoyed listening, not only because the stories gave her a glimpse into the life of a woman she'd always thought she'd known well, but also because of the excitement in her grandmother's voice. Dance had once been her love, and it seemed that emotion hadn't faded much over the years.

By the time they arrived back at the house, her grandmother's energy level had waned, her voice softening, her posture weakening. No sooner had they all walked in the door than she gave Cyr, Magus and Gina a hug and tottered off to bed, leaving the trio standing in the darkened living room. Alone.

Gina felt alive, exhilarated and much too awake to fall asleep. A little anxious, now that the distraction of her grandmother was gone.

She wasn't sure how to behave. She didn't want to send mixed messages. Last night had been beyond words. They'd made her feel so…alive. Beautiful. Wanted. Special. No man had ever made her feel this way before.

But all three of them had agreed last night was a once-only thing. And that was all. She was here for her grandmother. Period. Nothing or nobody else.

Chapter Six

ॐ

"Well, I guess that settles it, huh?" Gina giggled, her nervousness revealing itself. Still standing next to the front door, she shifted her weight from one foot to the other, pulled her wrap tighter around her shoulders. "We'll all be taking dance lessons if my grandmother has her way. But I want you to know I totally understand if you don't want to follow up or can't for whatever reason. My grandmother doesn't think about work schedules or other obligations—"

"Oh no." Cyr shot Magus a look Gina couldn't quite read. "I think we're both looking forward to the lessons. I had a great time tonight. Magus?"

"Yeah, me too. Though I'm not much of a dancer."

"Yet?" Gina added, trying like crazy to hide her jitters.

Magus' expression warmed. His lips curled into a stunner of a sly smile. "Yet. Though I'll have a hard time making it to lessons during game season."

"Believe me, I understand."

The conversation halted. Gina clenched her hands together, the ends of her wrap still wadded in her fists. Neither guy looked like he was ready to leave, but they hadn't moved deeper into the house either.

Could be because she hadn't invited them.

Should she invite them? Surely an innocent invitation wouldn't be misunderstood. Was it a crime if she enjoyed talking with them…looking at them…sitting near them…?

Just don't touch them.

She motioned toward the living room. "Um, would you like to come in for a while? To...talk about the kitchen repairs?"

"Sure." Cyr caught her hand and headed for the couch, taking her with him. "Let's talk about the kitchen."

Magus followed. Closely.

She sat, a guy on either side of her. Right away, she reclaimed her hand, folding it over the other and placing them in her lap. "So...what's next for the kitchen?"

"Relax." Magus set his hands on her shoulders and gently pulled until she was leaning against him.

So much for not touching them. Then again, to be technical, Magus was touching her. She'd kept her hands where they should be.

"There's still a lot of work that needs to be done." His gaze locked on her face, Cyr slowly pulled her wrap off. As it slid over her skin, tingles prickled over her arms and shoulders. Goose bumps followed.

Was he talking about the kitchen, or something else?

She stiffened. It was so unfair to lead these guys on. Yet their brand of seduction was so freaking powerful, she couldn't help herself. She could see what she was doing — saying no with her words but yes with her body, and she silently scolded herself for being so weak. "I'm going to have to buy some more comfortable shoes," she chattered. "For our dance class." Where was this weakness coming from? She was no swooning ninny. She'd always been able to lay down the law to a man and stick with it before.

Again, she wondered if it was because she wasn't kneeling in a dungeon, the rules all laid out in black and white like they usually were.

No rules. No clear-cut expectations. No escape clause.

"Yes, comfort is good." Magus' fingers worked the tight muscles knotted at the base of her skull.

"Are your feet hurting?" Cyr lifted one of her legs, unbuckled her shoe's strap and pulled it off.

"A little. These are the most comfortable dress shoes I own, but they're cheap. I can't wear them for long."

"Mmmmm." The kind, wonderful Cyr massaged her foot. Absolute heaven.

She closed her eyes and sighed. "Ohhh, now that feels amazing."

"So glad." He pulled off her other shoe. "These are sexy. They'd look better with a shorter skirt."

She opened her eyes, catching him giving her shoe a thorough once-over. "You're such a guy. Of course you'd say that," she teased. "Pervert." She wasn't about to admit she owned plenty of short skirts. The shortest ones barely covered her ass. She smoothed her hands down the material covering her thighs. "This was appropriate for tonight."

The truth was, she had all her sexy club clothes packed up in boxes and stored in her grandmother's basement, and they weren't coming out of storage. End of story. Why should they? She wouldn't be heading out to any clubs anytime soon.

"You'll wear the shorter one for our next date," Magus suggested.

Next date? Nonono.

Gina tried to sit up, but Magus wrapped a thick arm around her waist. A wave of erotic heat pumped through her body as she squirmed against his hold. "Um, I would but, like I tried to tell you last night, it's not practical for me to date right now. I can't leave my grandmother home alone—"

"We'll take care of that." Cyr set her shoe on the floor and tried to push the bottom of her skirt up to her knees. She stopped him. "We'll hire a nurse to stay with her. So if that's the only reason—"

"That's very nice, but really, I don't want to leave my grandmother. It's not so much a matter of logistics as it is

68

principles. She has done so many things for me over the years, I want to be here with her. It's my way of thanking her."

Magus loosened his hold on her waist. With his free hand, he cupped her cheek, coaxing her to turn her head toward him. "We can see you care for Isobel, but you need some time for yourself."

"It's not a crime," Cyr added. "You're young. You've set your life and needs aside. I know your grandmother will understand." His fingertips skimmed down the front of her shins. When he reached her ankles, he wrapped his hands around them tightly and pulled them apart.

A warm tingle erupted between her legs.

It was time to put a stop to this, before things went any farther. She wouldn't get busy here, now, in her grandma's living room, on her shiny gold and ivory brocade couch. With the curtains framing the big picture window open, so any passerby could see what was happening.

Granted, people didn't often stroll by. Her grandmother lived on a dirt road in a semi-rural area. But still, even with her exhibitionist tendencies, she didn't want her grandmother's neighbors to see this. She couldn't bring that kind of embarrassment to her grandma.

Not to mention, it plain wasn't right leading the guys on like this.

"Stop. Please." Giving Cyr an apologetic smile, she pushed her skirt down. "People can see —"

"Your bedroom then." Magus stood, taking her with him.

She dug her toes into the carpet and twisted her arm until her fingers slipped free. "No. I don't want you two to get the wrong idea."

"You mean you aren't attracted to us?" Cyr asked, looking slightly hurt.

"No, of course that's not what I meant." She motioned to both of them. "You're both gorgeous, and you know it too."

Magus gave a little nod of assent and snatched up her hand again. "Then you're not giving us the wrong idea."

Once more, she twisted her wrist, freeing her hand from Magus' grip. When he tried to grab it again, she crossed her arms over her chest and tucked her hands under her arms. "No, you're not listening. I can't start a relationship right now."

Magus cupped her face. Those dark eyes of his locked on hers. "We understand, Gina."

"Really, we do," Cyr agreed.

"No relationship," she stated, searching his face for any hint of reluctance.

Magus shook his head. "No commitment. We won't ask for more than you're able to give us right now, so you can concentrate on your grandmother."

"I don't know. It isn't very fair to ask you —"

Magus' smile was absolutely genuine. "We are perfectly happy to share whatever time you can for now."

So they were happy with the occasional no-strings sex. She supposed that would, indeed, make the average guy a happy camper. "Are you sure?"

"Absolutely. An hour here and there, when your grandmother is sleeping, if that's all you can spare right now, is perfectly fine. And we don't have to spend the time fucking, if you'd rather do something else. I just thought I'd make that clear. We're not total assholes, just looking for a convenient lay."

"But it's so one-sided —"

"Oh no it's not," Cyr interrupted. "We get plenty out of the time we spend together, no matter what we do when we're with you."

"You won't feel slighted? Or disappointed?"

"Never," Cyr stated matter-of-factly.

"Not at all," Magus said, sounding just as convincing. "Let us give you what you want, what you need, Gina. There's no reason for you to deny us. Companionship. Affection. Sex."

"Well..." She could find no argument against spending time together, as long as they both understood the situation. Although she felt slightly — very slightly — guilty for making them play by her rules. This was a first for her. "Okay."

"Good choice." In a blink, Magus had her thrown over his shoulder. He smacked her bottom.

She smiled as he hauled her down the hallway.

There'd been no pre-play interview, no discussion about limits or framework for the time she spent with these men. And while she'd become so accustomed to that kind of arrangement, and it was uncomfortable going without those security measures, she was beginning to enjoy the spontaneity this new thing with Magus and Cyr promised.

Crazy, what these two men had taught her about herself already.

Strangely, even though there was no dungeon, no formal declarations of position or power, the dynamic of this blossoming relationship still felt right. Although Cyr and Magus were kind, they emanated raw power. She felt their presence, always. They commanded her submission without ever speaking the words.

Maybe she didn't need a man who called himself her Master, but who simply was her Master. Who didn't tell her to get on her knees but inspired her to.

Cyr shut the bedroom door, closing them in her room, which was quickly becoming her place of darkly sweet secrets.

Magus let her down, but he still held her in his arms — strong, thickly muscled arms that possessed more brute strength than any that had held her before. He kissed her. Gently. Thoroughly. Lips, tongue and teeth performing a slow seduction.

Eyes closed, she focused on the glorious sensations, the way his fingertips ignited the nerves under her skin, the decadent flavor of his kiss, the heat of Cyr's body as he drew nearer.

Such wicked pleasure.

Two sets of hands peeled off her top. Skirt. Bra. Underwear. They explored her body, caressed, teased, tormented. They ignited tiny sparks in her blood with every stroke.

"We have been searching for you," Cyr whispered, the sound of his voice like a serenade. She didn't understand what he meant by those words, but the tone of his voice, the way it reverberated through her body, left her dizzy, clinging to Magus, and wobbly-kneed.

She whimpered and gradually relaxed her muscles, letting Cyr and Magus support her weight. How she ached for them to just take over, sweep her into their arms and carry her away. Tie her hands over her head, spread her legs and fuck her slow and easy and then hard and fast. "I've been searching too," she heard herself whisper, surprised by the confession.

Gently, they lowered her to the floor. Magus knelt on her left, closer to her shoulders. Cyr was on her right, down farther. Cyr ran his hands up her leg, fingernails grazing her skin to produce a sensual burn that made her writhe in ecstasy. She reached down, found his shoulders and hooked her fingers, clawing at cotton-covered concrete. Shoulders as hard as carved stone rippled and swelled beneath her hands as he moved.

Magus fondled her breasts, kneading, pinching, rolling nipples as sensitive as raw nerves. "We won't let you go now that we've found you," he promised. "We know that's what you want—to belong to us. To surrender everything, mind, body, soul."

The words drifted through her mind like the whisper of the wind through dry leaves. The other sensations were so much stronger, overpowering, distracting, yet those words echoed in her head.

She arched her back, lifting her breasts higher into the air. *Suck my breasts, please. Take me. I want to surrender.* She raised her arms, crossing her wrists over her head. It was a familiar position, comforting. Her way of saying what her mouth could not.

I'm yours.

Cyr pulled her knees apart, teased her labia with a finger. Her empty pussy clenched, heat thrumming, pulsing, pumping through her body.

Hands closed around her wrists, pinning them to the floor. Yes, she was under their control.

"My Masters," she whispered as she rocked her hips up, her body tight with expectation.

Cyr's finger slipped inside then immediately withdrew. Such a brief claiming. Too short. More. She craved more touches, strokes, inside. A thick cock pumping, hard, hands holding her. A thorough possession.

"More, please," she whispered.

Cyr shook his head, his index finger dragging across her labia. "You're going to have to earn our cocks this time."

A challenge. How fun. She knew how to play this kind of game, and better yet, it was a safe one. Grinning, she licked her lips. "Yes, Master. Tell me how."

Magus grabbed her chin, tilting it up. "We are not playing, Gina. This isn't a game."

Confused, she looked at him. Of course this was a game. It was always a game. What did he mean?

"You are not permitted to call us Master. Not yet."

"Okay." Even though she wasn't sure what was going on, a little thrill rippled through her. "I guess I misunderstood. I thought..." Embarrassed, she dropped her gaze to Cyr's flushed face. "I thought we were role playing."

Cyr flattened his hand over her hot center, the heel pressing against her thrumming clit. "No role playing. We'd rather be real."

"Yes, *real*. Instead of playing a game, we'll give you a test. To see how well you've been paying attention." Magus' fingers curled. His thumb stroked her lower lip, and out of reflex she relaxed her mouth. "You are so beautiful. When you can tell us what part of you we find most intoxicating, you'll have what you want."

She looked into his eyes, trying to read the truth, but all she saw there were dark shadows and mysteries. Hard masculine desire. What part would he say? Her face? He touched it a lot. Her breasts? He had given them more attention than any lover had before.

What part?

She looked to Cyr for a hint. He was now on his knees, waiting. Looking like he was in agony.

Magus' hand moved lower until it circled her neck. He didn't strangle her, there was no pressure. Yet his hold was firm. "Think, Gina. And remember what we said, this is not a game. We're not pretending. And this isn't just about this moment, or even tonight."

What did this mean then? Once again, she struggled with the lack of guidelines and rules, black and white explanations of what she should expect.

If they weren't playing, if this wasn't just about a temporary satisfaction, exorcizing of a drive, then what was it about?

"My...face?" she offered, taking a stab in the dark.

Magus shook his head. "No."

They were done for tonight. She could see it in their faces.

Cyr stood, and she snapped her legs closed.

Jerks! This was cruel. She wanted to smack them. Tell them they'd blown it, she didn't need this.

Not playing games? This was one of the most infuriating games any man had ever played with her. Yet something inside told her to wait, be patient. The struggle and uncertainty would be worth it. Maybe for once the reward would be worth the price.

She watched them leave, hoping they would come back tomorrow night but refusing to ask.

* * * * *

"You two look like hell." Sprawled on the couch, the remote in his fist and a beer in the other, Troi gave Magus and Cyr an amused glance. "Gina is hot. I wanted her the minute I saw her. But I'm glad it's you and not me." He pointed the remote at the television, and clicked through at least a dozen channels. "Some blessing."

"You want every woman you see." Cyr dragged his arm across his forehead, the sleeve saturated with sweat. "A few minutes of peace are worth hours of agony, you'll see."

"I don't want every woman I see, just the ones I can't have. And the ones I can." His expression souring, Troi shook his head. "I can't imagine anything being worth the hell you two are going through though." He motioned to Magus, who had staggered in behind Cyr, possibly more worn out and ravaged by Wrath than Cyr was. "Things were bad enough before but now look at him. The guy is losing control. It's getting worse."

"I'm fine," Magus growled, straightening up slightly. His face was deep scarlet, every muscle stretched taut, producing a mask of pain and fury. He walked stiffly to the bar and poured a drink, downing it in one gulp.

Amun wandered in, took one look at Cyr then Magus and shook his head. "How much longer are you two going to go on like this?"

"Until she's ready." Cyr decided a drink sounded damn good right now. Something that would burn in his gut and shut up the fucking beast. "She's obviously been to a dungeon before. But she thinks we're all about role playing."

Amun shrugged. "So give her what she wants. She'll love you anyway. That's all you need."

"No." Magus poured himself another drink and dumped it down his throat. "She won't. She'll respect us. She'll submit to us. But she won't love us."

It had been hell to leave Gina tonight. The moment they left her, the beast had roared within him, ripping at his spirit, shredding his sanity. Cyr couldn't think of anything but turning around and heading back into her room. Throwing her onto the bed and unleashing all his pent-up passion. But he didn't.

He couldn't break his promise, no matter how bad it was. Because he knew it was even harder on Magus.

Their plan was working. They weren't just fucking Gina. Taking their pleasure. Or playing the games they sensed she had played with other lovers. In their Gina, they could see the submissive who had been trained by other Doms.

Instead, they were taking her deeper. Beyond games, to a level they knew she longed to explore.

After emptying his glass, Cyr took yet another look at Magus. He looked like hell, but Cyr knew they were doing the right thing. "When the games stop, she can call us Master. Only then."

He dumped a second full shot of tequila down his throat and closed his eyes, silently praying it would calm the beast a little. Beside him, he heard Magus pour another for himself. He heard glass clanking against glass then glass thunking against the bar's counter and heavy footsteps retreating.

"I've had enough of you assholes for one night."

"Hey, Amun, take a look at this. Damn." Troi pointed at the television. "That's one fierce ride. We gotta get one."

Cyr poured one last shot, swallowed it in a single gulp and headed toward the stairs, grateful for the slight relief the alcohol had provided. Air moved in and out of his lungs more freely. The knot in his gut had loosened. Only slightly, but it was better than it had been. The beast's voice had softened to a muted rumble.

He found Magus in their room, sitting on the bed, his head tipped down, elbows on knees and forehead cradled in his hands.

Cyr sat beside him.

"I can't take this much longer," Magus said.

Cyr placed his hand on Magus' knee. Heat seemed to radiate from Magus' skin, like an iron. "I know."

"No, you don't." Magus lifted his head. In the dim light, it looked like his eyes were glowing, like light was seeping from his pupils. A deep ruby hue, the shade of blood. "I'm fighting. I'm...losing."

Cyr stared at that strange light glowing in Magus' eyes, and inside him the beast laughed. The haunting, evil sound echoed through him and goose bumps instantly coated his entire body. "You can't give up."

The light wasn't an illusion, it was a sign. Magus was telling the truth.

Wrath was winning.

What could he do to help Magus subdue it? They were so close now. On the verge of paradise. He couldn't lose Magus to the beast. Not after they'd waited so long.

"Yes, I can." His jaw clenched, Magus charged across the room, halting at the window. Facing away from Cyr, he dropped his head into his hands and curled his fingers into his hair. "Fuckfuckfuck."

"No, Magus. Goddamn it, you can't give up. Not now. Not when we're so close. " Scared he was about to watch the destruction of man he loved, Cyr ran to Magus, grabbed his arm and pulled. "Please, hold on. Let me help you. I want to help you."

Chapter Seven

෨

Magus whirled around, slamming into Cyr and flattening him against the wall. He thrust his arms out, caging Cyr's head between them, hands splayed on the wall. "What do you want—this?" He rocked his pelvis forward, grinding his burning cock against the thick bulge straining at the front of Cyr's pants.

Cyr's gaze darkened, lips curling into a taunting smile. "Oh yeah." Cyr shoved his arms up then out, knocking Magus' away, and pushed around him. "But not right now. Not when you're—"

"What?" Magus swallowed a growl of pleasure as he swiveled around to chase after Cyr.

Cyr loved to fuck hard. Fast. Rough. And so did he. But tonight, thanks to the heat Gina had stirred within him, the beast's voice wasn't a whisper, it was a roar. And as much as Magus wanted to pound his cock into Cyr's ass, he didn't trust himself not to hurt him.

Dammit, he needed relief. He hurt. Everywhere.

Burned.

"Come back here." Magus grabbed Cyr's arm and yanked, hard, forcing Cyr to turn toward him.

"No, dammit." Cyr drew back and punched him in the chin.

The blow sent him staggering back a step, two. Pain blazed through his head, blinding him for a split second. Inside him, the beast howled. When his vision returned, the world appeared in shades of red. Dark. Light. Blood red.

His heart slammed against his breastbone, each beat excruciating, the tempo out of control. He lunged toward Cyr, knocking him onto the bed, face down.

Kill him, the beast demanded.

"No." Magus curled his fingers into Cyr's hair. Cyr's neck lengthened as Magus pulled, forcing Cyr's head back. Cyr's eyes were fiery when they met his. Dark pleasure. Temptation.

Magus moved up, slanting his mouth over Cyr's. Cyr's tongue pushed into his mouth, a welcome invasion. This was a kiss like none he had ever experienced, a passion so intense it threatened to destroy him.

More.

He tugged, bringing Cyr's head farther back, giving him better access. The kiss deepened. Breaths mingled. Tongues lashed at each other like swords. It was a battle. A seduction. A possession. All three.

Cyr moaned into their joined mouths, twisting beneath Magus as the kiss continued. Magus pushed up on all fours, allowing Cyr to roll onto his back.

This time, it was Cyr who was the aggressor. He caught Magus' face in his hands and pressed harder into the kiss, until the pressure was almost painful, a good kind of torment that only heightened Magus' lust.

Magus broke the kiss. Breathless and burning, he ripped at Cyr's clothes, tearing his shirt. Smooth skin. Warm. Hard body. His.

Cyr surged up, doing the same to Magus.

Shirts. Pants. Underwear. They had to come off. He needed to feel warm skin. Cyr's strong hands all over his body. Chest. Stomach. Cock.

Cyr's body was about to combust, his blood searing, heart thumping so heavily it was almost painful, nerves ablaze.

The last scrap of clothing was torn away and they were both nude. It was both a relief and a torment. They knelt, facing each other, chest to chest. Their mouths met, lips touched, pressed harder. Magus' tongue slipped into Cyr's mouth, filling it with his sweet flavor. Cyr's heartbeat thumped harder, heavier as he curled his fingers around Magus' wrists, locking his fist around them.

"I'm so hard I want to scream," Cyr whispered into their joined mouths.

Magus jerked his wrists free, shoving Cyr's chest. He dropped onto all fours over Cyr, his head at Cyr's waist level. "Dammit, if you don't fuck me, I'm going to go insane."

Cyr's cock hardened at the suggestion, heat rushing to the tip then rippling back up to his testicles.

Magus clamped his fist around Cyr's burning rod and gave it several slow swipes, applying just the right amount of pressure.

Cyr's eyes practically rolled back into his head. He closed them, allowing himself to focus on his other senses. The taste of Magus still lingering on his lips. The racing thump of his heart against his rib cage. The soft whisking sound of skin brushing skin as Magus stroked his cock. The building waves of need surging within him.

"I don't know what I'd do without you," Magus said, levering himself lower over Cyr. His tongue flicked across the tip of Cyr's cock, and Cyr's hips surged forward. "You keep me human. From losing it, buckling under the pressure of the beast." His moist lips slipped over the tip of Cyr's penis and he sucked, drawing Cyr deeper into the warm, wet depth. Into paradise.

Cyr groaned his gratitude. "Your love gives me the strength to keep fighting the beast too. You're my salvation. My hope. My world." He rocked his hips back and forth, fucking Magus' mouth. Deeper. Faster. Harder.

It didn't take long to bring him to the crest, not with Magus sucking him so hard. His muscles pulled tight. Arms. Shoulders. Stomach. Legs. Even his feet. Climax churned inside, like molten rock bubbling to the surface of the earth. Creeping closer. Closer yet. But before he came, he shoved Magus away, shouting, "No. Not this time." He pushed to his knees, crawled across the bed and reached for the lube sitting on the nightstand. Then he handed the tube to Magus. "Take your release, Magus."

The blood red light in Magus' eyes flickered one last time and then extinguished, like a spark drifting on a nighttime breeze. He kissed Cyr, sweetly this time, gently, patiently then spread some lube over Cyr's anus, testing the ring of muscle with a fingertip before replacing it with the tip of his cock. "I was so close to losing myself."

"Yes." Cyr relaxed as Magus eased into him. His body accepted his thick girth, his anus stretching.

Glorious fullness.

"I was an asshole." Magus' fingertips dug into the flesh of Cyr's hips as he eased almost completely out then slid back inside.

"Oh no, you weren't. But you are now."

"Am I going too slow?" Laughter lifted Magus' voice. His pace sped up. "I wouldn't want to be accused of being an unkind lover."

"Yes you would. You pride yourself on your cruelty."

"As best you know."

"And Gina. How you torment her."

"Guilty as charged. But I don't hear either of you complaining." Magus raked his fingers down Cyr's back, the bite of fingernails a welcome pleasure-pain. Cyr's breath caught in his throat. A sharp quake surged through his body. "Mmmm, that is so fucking hot. I love the way your body responds to my touch." Magus leaned lower, reaching around Cyr to close his fist around Cyr's rigid cock.

"And I love the way you touch me."

Magus tightened his hold on Cyr's cock, hand gliding up to the base then back down to the tip, over and over, in time with his thrusts into Cyr's ass.

Together, the sensations drove Cyr to the brink of orgasm once more. Heat whirled within his body like swirling storm clouds. Little mini-blasts of heat shot up his spine, like bolts of lightning. He trembled, rocking himself back and forth, forcing Magus' possession to deepen, quicken.

"Yes, yes! Like that," Cyr whispered. The telltale flare of dark heat shot up his chest.

Magus, reaching his own climax, roared, filling the room with the sound of his voice. The air grew heavy with the scent of sex and man and lust.

Absolute bliss. Complete release. Cyr catapulted over the crest, joining his lover on the other side.

Peace.

Relief.

Paradise.

Only one thing—person—would make this moment more precious. Gina. Here, by his side, her soft body molded to his. *Soon. We won't have to wait much longer.*

＊ ＊ ＊ ＊ ＊

"What are you watching, dear?" Gina's grandmother shuffled into the family room, rubber-soled slippers dragging across the carpet with a soft scuff, scuff sound. Like most days, she was wearing a pair of elastic-waisted polyester pants and a busy tunic top with a drawstring at the neck. Grandma wear. Her hair was combed into a knot at the base of her skull but tiny wisps stuck out around her face, too short to stay back.

"It's just an old football game. I'll turn on something you like." Gina lifted the remote, prepared to change the channel.

"Wait. Is this last year's Super Bowl?"

"Yup." She gave her grandma a double take. Her grandmother loved reality shows. Most of the day the television was tuned to the Fox Reality channel, where she could watch such bizarre and disturbing programs as *My Bare Lady*, *The Search for the Next Elvira* and *Battle of the Bods*. "Why?" This was the woman who had once lamented her husband watching football, calling it the devil's sport.

Gina had pretty much inherited her grandmother's attitude toward the sport too. But out of curiosity, she'd started watching this game after realizing Magus was playing. It was odd watching him as he worked. He was so aggressive on the field. So different from the way he was around her.

"Leave it on, sweetheart. I'd like to watch for a while."

"Okay." Gina set the remote on the table next to her grandmother's chair and headed toward the kitchen. "Do you want your usual for breakfast?"

"No, I think I'm in the mood for something different. I'm starving. How about some eggs, potatoes and meat?"

"All that? And meat?" Gina took a second long look at her grandmother. The woman hadn't consumed more than a toddler's portion of a meal in months. Where did this enormous appetite come from?

"Yes, I have a taste for some beef. Do we still have those steaks in the freezer?"

"Sure." Bewildered about her grandmother's odd behavior, Gina turned around and headed for the basement stairs, situated on the other side of the family room, next to the entry to the garage. Football. Now a breakfast fit for an athlete. She wondered if her grandmother's medications were to blame. Again.

She clomped down the wooden stairs and headed over to the chest freezer in the basement's corner, stocked with all kinds of foods. She found a steak, wrapped in heavy plastic, a date printed neatly in her grandmother's handwriting.

"It's going to take a while for this to thaw." Gina dropped the frozen block of meat on the counter. It landed with a sharp thunk. "It's hard as a rock. How about I cook it for lunch instead?"

"Oh, that's too bad. But I suppose it won't kill me to wait. All right." Her grandmother sighed then let out a whoop. "That man has magic hands! Did you see that catch?"

"Magic, you say?" Gina smiled to herself as she reached into the refrigerator. Eggs. Butter. Cheese. Ham. She had the makings of a scrumptious omelet. That should satisfy her grandmother's appetite.

"That young man of yours can run. Look at him go!"

"He's not mine, Grandma." Gina set a frying pan on the burner, turned on the power and dropped a pad of butter into it.

"Of course he is. Don't be silly. You have both of those boys wrapped around your little finger." Her grandmother extended her pinky to illustrate. "Just like I did years ago."

"Do you mean Grandpa?" Gina asked, stirring the butter to make it melt.

"Oh no. He was the one who wouldn't let me catch him. Or at least not at first. That was why I had to have him."

"Ah, I see now." As she stared down at the simmering butter, she imagined her grandmother as a young woman, flirting with her grandfather, who had always been somewhat aloof, even into his final days. But boy did her grandma ever love the man.

It looked like something besides blue eyes and a predisposition for diabetes ran in the family.

Just like her grandma, she could not resist the allure of strong men who didn't wear their hearts on their sleeves. Men who were unattainable. Hard to read. Mysterious, with a hint of bad boy in them. That was the kind of guy she'd always gone for too. Which was why she was so surprised by how intensely she had reacted to Magus and Cyr. They were strong men. Powerful. But they were more open.

Or were they? Honestly, what did she know about them? When she thought about it she realized they hadn't shared much about themselves. It was more like...they were drawing her out. By keeping her guessing what they would do next.

Interesting.

Gina dropped two slices of bread into the toaster. "Actually, Grandma, I think it's kind of the other way around. They have me wrapped around their little fingers."

Her grandmother gave her a long, hard look. "Then it's very much like your grandfather." She smiled, eyes sparkling. "I'm glad. I know you'll be happy after I'm gone."

"Grandma. Please don't talk like that."

Her grandmother shook her head. "There's no reason to avoid talking about it. I will die eventually."

Her grandmother's words had Gina rushing to her side. Gina gently scooped her grandmother's little hand into hers. So delicate. Heavy wrinkled, every vein visible through the paper-thin skin. "Please stop. You're still very strong. My gosh, at the dance studio, you outdance people half your age."

Her grandmother set her free hand on top of Gina's. "Sweet girl. I know my time is almost up. I feel it in every bone. I've held on for you. Or maybe it was my own foolish selfishness. I wanted this time with you. But I'm tired."

Gina's nose burned. Her eyes too. She didn't know what to say. In between the words, she heard a very different, troubling statement—her grandma felt she was a burden. "I love you. I'm happy we have this time together."

Her grandmother's answering smile was wistful. "I love you too, my sweet girl." She let go of Gina's hand and pointed toward the kitchen. "But you better go mind the stove before we have another fire."

The smell of smoke suddenly singed her nostrils. Gina gave a yelp and spun around. "Oh no!"

Chapter Eight

ɞ

"I think I'll head to bed."

"Grandma? It's only six-thirty." Worried, Gina started toward her grandmother, but the feisty woman shooed her away. Her grandma been acting strangely all day, but not in a bad way. Normally, Gina had to coerce her into eating enough food to keep a child half her size alive. Not today. She'd been perkier than usual, too. She'd even ventured outside for a stroll down to the end of the street and back. "Did that walk wear you out?"

Her grandmother scowled. "Walk? Not at all. I can go more than fifty yards without collapsing."

"I'm sorry, Grandma, I didn't mean—"

"Now you just go watch some TV. Leave me be. I'm fine. I just want to relax. In private."

How strange. In private?

Gina had a feeling there was more to this than her grandma needing some rest and solitude. The crafty woman looked as perky as a toddler on a sugar high. She was no more tired than she had been at twelve noon. And she hated being alone.

But her grandmother left Gina no option but to puzzle over her continuing odd behavior as she watched her shuffle down the hallway.

Then there was a knock on the front door, putting an end to Gina's bewilderment. She smiled and headed for the living room, recalling the phone call she'd missed this morning when she'd been in the shower. Her grandma had told her it was a sales call, nobody important.

That little liar.

Gina peered out the window. Sure enough, Magus and Cyr stood on the porch, dressed in jeans and t-shirts. They looked rather strained though, faces tight, color deep. Something had to be wrong. She yanked open the door. "Is everything okay?"

"Fine." Cyr grinned.

Magus nodded. "Yep. Why?"

Strange, but their expressions were suddenly as carefree as a kid's on a warm summer day. "You look—looked—a little tense before..." She stepped to the side to let both men in.

"Ah." Cyr brushed past her, a breeze of cologne-scented air following him. It was a unique scent, as unusual as its wearer. Spicy. Masculine. Addictive. "I see you've drawn my grandma into your schemes."

They each gave her a totally unconvincing puzzled expression. Terrible actors, both of them.

"What schemes?" Magus leaned over and kissed her on the cheek. It was a sweet gesture, old-fashioned, charming. And it produced an old-fashioned reaction in her—a pitter-pattery heart flutter.

"Even if we were guilty of a little harmless scheming, you'd be more than willing to forgive us, wouldn't you?" Cyr hinted, big puppy dog eyes pleading.

"After all, we haven't been unkind," Magus added.

"Oh good grief! Okay, okay. Who could stay mad at you two for more than a minute?" She threw her arms around Cyr's neck and gave him a hug. He returned it with equal enthusiasm. Then she hugged Magus. The way he held her stirred a different kind of reaction in her body. A tense sensation as if her nerves were being pulled tight. But it wasn't an uncomfortable feeling at all. In fact, she really liked it. A lot.

Despite her frustration last night, she was so glad they were here. Ridiculously happy. On the verge of over-the-moon joy. Just looking at those faces, hearing their voices, it was wonderful. Better than wonderful. Jeesh, she was getting sappy. She really did need to get a life.

Forcing herself to let go of Magus, she stepped back. "Ready to get to work?" Trying not to look too desperately happy to see them, she motioned toward the kitchen. "I'm assuming that's the reason for the visit, right?"

"You mean we have to have a reason?" Cyr teased before taking her hand and heading toward the kitchen in his usual slow, loose-hipped gait. The man might have earned the nickname "Bullet" on the ice, but on dry earth, he moved at a sure but slow pace. A man who was in no hurry to go anywhere but had the strength and agility to haul ass when needed. "Just joking. We're ready." He released her hand, fingertips touching hers for a split second, and then he was gone, having followed Magus into the garage.

She slumped onto the couch, kicked up her feet and snatched up the book she had been reading, toying with the curled edge at the corner as she stared at the page. She was too distracted to read. Too distracted to do anything but stare blindly at the TV and listen to the thumping and clanging out in the garage. In her head, images of the past few nights with her pair of handymen-slash-dance-partners-slash-lovers played over and over. Last night, writhing beneath her tormentors, practically begging for their touch. The magical moment she'd shared with Cyr at the dance school. The first time she'd seen Magus, after her grandmother had wandered into their house.

How long had it been since she'd met them? A month? Not even close. A week? Not yet. She knew very little about Cyr and Magus, outside of what they did for a living. And yet she already felt the connection she shared with them deepening.

Tonight, she was determined to learn more, the silly but intimate things that casual sex partners wouldn't know about each other. If they were going to pull her into an intimacy she hadn't been prepared for, she was going to return the favor. So there.

Magus entered first, carrying a power drill and a bunch of tools. "What're you reading?" he asked as he passed, eyes flicking first to the book and then to her face.

"Oh, it's..." What had she been reading? God, she'd read almost half of the book, yet the title was gone, lost from her memory, probably because the gray matter had decided there were more important things to attend to, like how Magus' butt looked in those jeans. She glanced down, eyes skimming across the cover. *Oh yeah. Ohhhh.* For a split second, she hesitated in saying the title aloud, but then she quickly reasoned that it was very unlikely either he or Cyr would be familiar with the author's books. "*Demon's Fire* by Emma Holly."

"Interesting." Magus pulled one of the empty drawers from the base cabinet and set it on the floor. "Is this the first Emma Holly book you've read?"

"Yeah. I found it at the library and thought I'd give it a try. I, uh, liked the cover." Cheeks warming, she toyed with the curled corner as she watched him somehow cram the better part of his upper body into a base cabinet. "Where's Cyr?"

"He went up to the store for supplies." One of Magus' arms appeared from the cabinet. He reached blindly for something.

Gina dropped the book and hurried over to him. "What're you looking for?"

"Screwdriver."

"Got it." She set it in his hand then moved just far enough away to let him work while staying near enough to help if needed. "So, have you read any books by Emma Holly?" It was a silly question, she knew. Men didn't read steamy romance novels. Especially men like Magus and Cyr—manly men's-men. They probably read sports magazines.

"Yep. I've read everything she's had published."

Okay, so she'd been wrong. Which meant he knew what kind of book it was. Bisexual demons doing the naughty. Her cheeks grew even hotter.

Oh this was silly. First, he just admitted he read that kind of book too. And second, he'd seen her naked and she'd shared some of the most intense sensual moments of her life with this man.

Magus poked his head out from the cabinet. "You got mighty quiet."

"Yeah. I guess you took me by surprise, admitting you've read romance novels. I've never met a guy who read anything but the newspaper or *Popular Mechanics* before."

"That you know of."

"True. Some are probably secret in-the-closet romance fans."

"Like Cyr. He reads them too, but he'd never admit it."

"That just blows me away."

"Why?"

"Because...I don't know. It just does."

Magus shook his head in a show of disapproval but the expression on his face said something else entirely. "You women want to keep all those hot stories to yourselves, don't you? Your naughty little secret." He crawled on hands and knees toward her, eyes glimmering, muscles rippling. Closer he came, closer still. He reminded her of a lion, strong and noble and majestic. Fierce. His arm extended, and just as he was about to grab her hand, he swung his arm to the side and snatched a hammer instead. "Gotcha." He winked.

"No, you didn't get me." She pressed her thighs together, all too aware of the tingling between them.

"You thought I was going to do something else, didn't you? Just like you thought you knew what I was going to say. I'm not that predictable." He ducked back into the cabinet.

"As I'm learning." Gina scooted closer on her butt, her jeans sliding over the textured vinyl floor. "But my lack of knowledge about you isn't entirely my fault. You and Cyr haven't told me much about yourselves. I know your names. I know your jobs, and I know you're both pretty damn good dancers. But that's it."

"First, I wouldn't call what I do on the dance floor *dancing*." He poked his head out again. "I'm not too proud to admit my dance skills are pretty damn lacking. Second, ask me anything and I'll answer." Before she responded, he tucked his shoulders and head back into the cabinet.

She stared at what parts of his body she could see, which was most of it, and admired it as she puzzled about what to ask first. "Okay. I've got one. What is the nature of your relationship with Cyr? Are you just roommates? Friends?" *Lovers?* "How did you two meet?"

"That's technically more than one question. But I'll answer. Cyr and I met a very long time ago. We were introduced by a mutual acquaintance and we have lived together for a long time, first as friends, later as *partners*." He emphasized the last word.

So they shared more than kisses. Images of their bodies twined, arms and legs tangled, flashed through her mind. What a glorious sight that would be, those two beautiful men touching, caressing, giving and taking pleasure.

She'd watched gay men fuck before. Ironically, when she was in college, her two best friends had been gay. One night, when she was spending the night at their house, she saw them making love. In the living room. It was late, and clearly they figured she was asleep. That sight was burned into her memory forever. Sadly, it changed her relationship with them somehow, and months later her friendship with them deteriorated. She had wanted them, as more than friends. She wanted to be a part of the intimate moments they shared late at night, when everyone else was asleep.

How strange that now it seemed she might find her chance to share just that kind of relationship. These guys weren't Jason and Alec. They were very different.

They were strong. Athletic. Powerful. And dominant without slapping leather on their bodies and pretending to be someone else.

They were real.

They were perfect.

Magus pushed his way out of the cabinet and sat facing her. "You got quiet again."

"Yeah. I was thinking."

"About?"

"Some friends I had back in college. Nothing important."

Magus scooted toward the next cabinet. "Almost done. Once I get all the screws holding the counter out, I can pull it up. Cyr should be back with the new one soon." He gave her a smile. "No more questions? You've let me off pretty easy."

"Oh I'm not done yet."

"Fair enough." He ducked into the cabinet.

Over the clank and thunk and clatter he made, she said, "This is awkward, but I need to ask. I'm guessing both you and Cyr are bisexual. Have you shared lovers before?"

"Nope. You're our first."

"Really?" She wondered why that was, and she marveled at the suggestion she read into that three-word sentence.

"Yep."

More clanking followed, and she hesitated asking more questions, because of the noise.

"Shit, the screw's stripped." Magus' chest visibly rose and fell. A sigh of frustration, probably. "I'm down to the last one, and it's not moving. Just my luck."

"Sorry."

"It's not your fault." He dragged himself out. This time, as his upper body emerged, his face was deep scarlet, she guessed from exertion.

She blurted, "Why haven't you shared a lover before? Why me?"

"It's a bit complicated. The best way to explain it is to say we both recognized something very special in you, and once we did, we couldn't stay away." He took her hand.

She stared down at his tapered fingers and tried to imagine those hands catching and throwing a football, but even though she'd watched him on TV, she couldn't. It was like that man on the television was someone else. And all she'd ever seen those hands do was touch her, caress her, pleasure her. "Things seem to be happening so fast. It's hard to keep it casual."

"Are you scared?"

"No." When he didn't say anything else, she asked, "You?"

"Not at all. I've been waiting a long time for this. I am genuinely happy."

"Waiting? Why? Weren't you happy with Cyr?"

"Very much so. But both of us knew someday we would find a third, a woman, who would make us complete."

Having never been in such a complicated relationship, she couldn't fully appreciate what he meant by that, but she nodded as if she understood. These two men loved each other, but for some reason she couldn't grasp, that wasn't enough. They'd been waiting for a woman. And now it seemed they'd decided she was this woman, the one who would make them "complete".

This wasn't a casual thing they were looking for.

She had to set them straight. "Right now, I need to focus on my grandmother. And once she's —" She couldn't speak the word aloud so she searched for words she could say. "When my grandmother is gone, I'm going back. To my life. My job. I can't stay here forever. I'm sorry if that's what you were thinking."

He gave her a look. Nodded. "We told you we were willing to follow your lead. I'm not going to push you into anything. Neither will Cyr."

She wanted to believe him. The muffled sound of a car door slamming wrenched her attention away from Magus for a moment. By the time she looked his way again, he was on his feet.

She followed him. Before either of them reached the door leading out to the garage, it opened, and Cyr stepped inside. He looked exhausted. Or maybe he was in pain. She didn't know which. "Are you okay?"

"Fine now." Cyr plopped onto the couch's arm, bracing his arms against his thighs. He audibly inhaled several times, in, out, in, out, as if he'd sprinted a mile.

"Are you sure? Can I get you something to drink?"

"No thanks. I'm fine." He exchanged tense looks with Magus. "Had a little trouble at the Home Depot."

One of Magus' brows lifted. "Oh yeah?"

They exchanged another look, and Gina could practically see the tension in the air. It was like fog in a very dark, moonless night. Cool fingers of damp air brushing over her skin. A chill crept up her spine.

Cyr jerked a thumb over his shoulder. "The new countertop is out in the truck. Are you ready for it?"

"Not quite. I had some trouble with a stripped screw."

"We can drill it out."

"Good idea." Magus headed toward the garage. "I'll get the drill and load it up with the right bit."

"Okay. I'll get a look at what you ran into." Cyr's attention moved to Gina. He looked like he wanted to say something.

Curious, she waited, hands clasped. She smiled, a silent encouragement.

"I guess I'd better get in the kitchen." He rested a hand on her shoulder as he stepped past her. His gaze locked on her face. One step, two. She pivoted, watching him, but instead of speaking, he let his hand drop and moved toward the cabinets.

What was that all about?

Cyr lifted one corner of the counter.

"The stuck screw is down in that corner." She pointed toward the far end.

He nodded. "Thanks." Seemingly focused on the task at hand, he moved down to the cabinet in question, knelt and wedged his shoulders into the narrow cabinet opening. "What a mess."

"Are you going to be able to get it?"

"Sure. As soon as Magus brings the drill."

As if on cue, Magus entered from the garage, a cordless drill in his hand. He handed it to Cyr then, as the whirr of the drill filled the room, he moved to the free end of the counter.

Seconds later, or so it seemed, the sound of drilling stopped.

"That ought to do it." Cyr wiggled out of the tight opening and together he and Magus lifted off the scarred counter and carried it through the family room. Gina rushed ahead of them, opening the door to the garage so they could carry it out. They dropped it on the concrete, measured it, and marked the new one—ten times nicer than the original.

Gina felt helpless, watching them work.

She felt useless while watching them cut the counter. She felt useless while watching them carry it inside. And she felt useless while watching them install it.

Finally, when they were finished, she hoped she wouldn't feel useless anymore.

"Done for tonight." Magus dropped onto the couch, grabbed Gina by the waist and hauled her down onto his lap. He nuzzled her neck. "I didn't tell you earlier, but you smell good." His voice was a low rumble, sexy and masculine.

"Thanks. So do you." She wasn't lying. He did smell good. Like man and fresh air.

Cyr rested his butt on the couch's armrest, tossed an arm over her shoulders and pulled her toward him. He kissed her, and she kissed him back. It was a slow, sensual kiss. Tender and expressive. A seduction rather than a ravishment. She thoroughly enjoyed every second of it. A sigh of contentment slipped past her lips.

When he broke the kiss, he rested his forehead against hers. "What did you two do while I was gone?"

"Worked," Magus answered, sounding a little defensive. "There had to be at least two dozen screws holding that old counter down. Talk about overkill."

Cyr pulled away, piercing eyes focused on hers. "Is that true?"

"Sure."

He grinned, letting her know he was fooling around. "If I'd been the one to stay, I wouldn't have worked the whole time."

"That's why you went and I stayed." Magus' voice was light with laughter, eyes sparkling with fun. "You have the willpower of a sugar addict in a chocolate factory."

"Well, can you blame me?" Cyr cupped Gina's chin, traced her lower lip with an index finger. "Look at this decadent little morsel. I can't get enough of her."

"I hear you, but remember what we talked about."

Cyr scowled.

Magus patted her thigh and she twisted at the waist.

"What's up?" she asked. Nothing like being the only one in the room who wasn't in on The Big Secret.

"It's not that big a deal. We just want to give you more space. Like you said yourself, things have been going fast, and you have some things to sort out..." He gently forced her to her feet.

"Are you leaving?" Good grief, she sounded way too desperate. "I mean, thanks for installing the new cabinets and countertop. My grandmother and I both appreciate it."

"No problem." Magus stood, shooting Cyr a glance. "Ready?"

Cyr didn't look happy to be going. "Yeah." He caught her fingertips in his as he slowly shuffled toward the door. "Good night, Angel." He lifted her hand, brushed his mouth over the back. A gallant gesture. Sweet. Romantic. Sigh-inducing.

She barely got the words, "Good night," out before they were through the doorway. They each gave her one last smile then turned and headed out into the dark night.

Talk about a total letdown, although the night wasn't a total wash. She'd learned a little about Magus and Cyr.

And now that they were gone, she was learning a little about herself too. She was a sucker for a man who was playing hard-to-get.

"I have a lot to teach you, I see," her grandmother scolded.

"Grandma?" Gina glanced over her shoulder to find her standing in the hallway behind her, scowling. "I thought you were sleeping."

"You are a terrible dancer and know nothing about seducing a man. How can I leave you, knowing you're in such sad shape?"

"I'm not in sad shape at all."

"Keep telling yourself that and maybe someday you'll believe it."

Gina laughed. Only her grandmother would say something like that. And only from her grandmother could she accept such criticism without being hurt. It had taken her years to learn how to take the woman's in-your-face bluntness, but eventually she had. "Did we wake you up?"

"Naw, I wasn't asleep. I finished my book. Awful ending. I'll never buy another book by that author again. I can't stop thinking about it. She killed the hero. In a romance novel. That simply shouldn't be done. Do you want to watch a little television with me?"

"Sure." She took her grandmother's hand to help her walk.

"While we're watching, I'll give you a few pointers on how to handle those two rascals. They're a fiery pair. There's only one way to handle men like that…"

* * * * *

Cyr's world was dark. Hell. Shadows. Pounding heat. Fury so intense his skin was instantly slicked with sweat. Burning. Everywhere. So close to losing control. He stumbled and fell onto the wet grass. "I can't take any more of this game, Magus."

"She's not ready," Magus whispered breathlessly.

"You're sure?"

"Yeah. Positive. Especially after tonight. All she can give us yet is a superficial submission, pretend, make believe, counterfeit. We need her love and trust first. Then she will fully submit."

"Damn the gods. Why do they make us suffer when we're so fucking close to redemption?"

"It's not the gods." Magus shook him. "You know it's true. As long as we let her hide behind a façade of submission, she'll never be ours."

"Can't go on. Must do…" A fresh blaze of anger raced through him. Cyr stood and started running again, leg muscles aching, lungs starved for air. Still he couldn't stop. The beast inside was shrieking now, demanding blood. Demanding release. And he could no longer deny it. His will was gone, the last tendrils snapping like a thread pulled too tight.

Who would silence Wrath? How?

Somehow, he had to defeat it now. This second. Before the beast swallowed the tiny piece of his spirit that remained.

Magus, the beast whispered. *It's his fault.*

"No."

Yes. His fault. He told her too much. Now she doesn't want you.

"No."

It's true. You know it. Look how he pushed her last night. His fault.

Tears streamed from his eyes, blinding him. "Leave me alone. Let me die." He pressed his hands over his ears and pushed himself, running harder, muscles burning, pain blazing through his body. His insides twisted into excruciating knots. His lungs burned with the need for air. Still he didn't stop, couldn't. He propelled himself forward, hoping something big and hard would plow into him and finally stop the torment.

The monster kept shouting those words, and he didn't want to hear them. But with each footstep, every thump of his heart, the beasts' words became more convincing. Until he knew they were true.

Dammit, it was Magus' fault he was in such agony. Where was the motherfucker?

Cyr spun around and sprinted back toward the house, the words, *his fault, his fault,* pounding through his head with every agonizing step he took. Down the dark street, across the lawn. *There.* Cyr stopped, spying Magus crouching low, eyes glowing red.

"What have you come for? A taste of blood?" Magus snarled. "The only blood that'll be spilled tonight will be yours." Magus leapt into the air, arms stretched in front of him, red eyes fixed on Cyr.

Cyr braced for the inevitable impact. It came. Bones cracked. He felt nothing. The sound of fists pounding, breath sawing in and out of air-starved lungs, guttural growls. His head snapped back. He threw his fists, blindly punching.

"What the hell? Oh shit!" someone yelled. "Rane! Amun! Get out here."

A woman's scream. Gina.

His blood turned to ice, and his rage evaporated instantly. Something slammed into his face, and his vision went completely black.

Another scream.

"Come on, you bastard." That was Delius. "You two gotta stop, before someone gets hurt."

"Where's Gina?" Still blind, Cyr tried to fight out of Delius' grip.

"She's home, which is good. I doubt you'd want her to see you like this."

Something wet dripped down his forehead. He lifted his hand to wipe it away. His fingers moved stiffly and his arm was heavy. And he still couldn't see anything. "Can't see."

"That's because your eyes are swollen shut." Delius heaved an audible sigh. "You two messed each other up pretty damn good. I'd hate to see what might've happened if we hadn't stopped you. You might've killed each other."

"We couldn't be so lucky," Magus said from somewhere close by.

Chapter Nine

છ

Gina slammed the door and fell back against it. Tiny blinking stars obscured her vision. Red. Gold. Silver. She blinked, frantically trying to clear them away.

Whatthehell, whatthehell, whatthehell?

"They'll be okay. It looked worse than it was." The man standing next to her gave her shoulder a pat. "Um, do want me to get you a glass of water? You should sit down."

"Yes," she answered, not certain what she was responding to. Did she want water? Or did she want to sit down? She let the man help her across the living room. He turned her and something soft bumped the back of her legs.

"There you go. Have a seat. I'll be back in a sec."

She bent her legs, letting herself plop onto the couch, and covered her face with trembling hands.

What the hell had she'd seen outside? Cyr and Magus, on their front yard, pounding each other with their fists, eyes glowing red, like a cat's, faces contorted into masks so hideous she barely recognized them.

No. She'd seen nothing. Yeah, that was it. She was asleep right now, having a nightmare. Yes, a nightmare. She pulled in a long, deep breath and slowly let it out.

At least the stars seemed to have faded. A good sign.

"Here you go." It was a male voice, the man who'd walked her home. One of the guys who lived next door. She didn't remember his name.

"I'm going to wake up any minute now and this nightmare'll be over. Right?"

"Uh, sure."

She slowly peeled her fingers away from her face and tipped her head in the direction of his voice. He was holding a glass of water, looking like he had no clue what to do next. "Thanks." She accepted it, took a sip and handed it back to him.

With his free hand, he patted her shoulder. "So you're okay now, right? You're not going to pass out or anything?"

"I'm pretty sure."

"Good." He set the glass on the side table, next to her grandma's prize Capodimonte piece. "I'd better get back to the house. Gotta check on Cyr and Magus."

"What happened? Are they going to be okay?"

"Oh yeah, they'll be fine. Like I said, it looked worse than it was. Don't worry."

"Okay. Thanks for walking me home. I wasn't feeling very good there for a few minutes."

"Not a problem." He gave her one last look then stood up. "I'll see myself out. Don't get up."

She stood anyway and regretted it immediately.

* * * * *

"Thanks for checking on Gina. How is she?" Magus didn't wait for Rane to step into the room before asking. Since he'd been hauled inside, he couldn't stop thinking about her, worrying about what she'd seen, what she might be thinking.

Rane gave a little shrug. "Shaken up, but she'll be okay."

Magus scrubbed his hands over his aching, bruised face, his fingers pressing lightly at the sorest spot, above his left eye. "Does she hate us?"

"I don't think so."

"Fear us?"

"Possibly. I think she's confused."

"Maybe I should go talk to her." Magus pushed against the mattress, propelling himself to his feet.

Rane forced him back down. "I think it would be better if you didn't go anywhere right now. What happened out there? You two have never fought like that."

Magus curled his fingers into the silk coverlet, the cool fabric warming almost instantly. "It was the beast. I couldn't hold it back."

"It made you turn on Cyr?" Looking confused, Rane crossed his arms over his chest.

Magus knew why Rane looked confused. For the same reason he was. The beast had whispered a lot of despicable things into his head, tempted him to do heinous things, but never had it allowed him to hurt Cyr. Belt him once or twice when he deserved it, sure. But never pound the life out of him. "Yeah."

"The dark spirits have been getting stronger. All of us are feeling different, as if the darkness is progressively spreading though our bodies like a cancer. Eating away what little good we have left in us. But they haven't made any of us turn on each other before. Not that you two didn't argue in the past. We all have. But you'd never fought like that. I wonder why? What's happening to you? To all of us?"

"I wonder too." This time it was confusion that propelled him to his feet. And unlike the last time, this time Rane didn't force him back down. Magus walked to the window and pulled aside the curtain. "Maybe I forced it to turn on him, because I wouldn't hurt someone else—a mortal." Weary and worried, he sighed as he let the curtain fall closed again. He leaned back against the wall and mirrored Rane's crossed arms. "All I do know is that it's getting stronger every time we leave Gina. We've both been struggling, but we've been able to keep it under control. Until tonight."

"I guess it's a good thing it was Cyr then. You two could've picked a better place to fight though. Around here, people call the cops when they see two assholes using each other as punching bags."

"I'm sorry. For the trouble it caused. Not to mention Gina saw us, which could be a bigger problem." His head slumped forward, and no matter how hard he tried, he couldn't find the strength to lift it. "We're both hanging on by a thread."

"What are you saying?"

"I didn't know the spirit could destroy us. I thought we were safe. But I don't believe that anymore. It's so much stronger now." He paused a beat, meeting Rane's troubled gaze. "I'm scared."

"Shit." Rane sat on the bed and, elbows on his bent knees, stared down at the floor. After what seemed like forever, he said, "Now might be a good time to tell Gina the truth."

"She wouldn't believe the truth. She needs more time to get to know us, to feel comfortable. She's dealing with some stuff too. We have to give her a chance to work through that. She won't be ready for anything until she does."

"But what if next time it's a mortal you attack? What if you kill someone?"

"Believe me, I've asked the same question. We have to take precautions."

"What precautions? Delius, Amun, Troi and I can't follow you two 24/7."

"I know."

"Then what're you thinking?"

"To keep everyone safe, you're going to have to lock us up immediately after we leave her. At least for a few hours, longer if necessary."

"Lock you? Where?"

"I don't care. Chain us to our beds. Strap us in straitjackets. Do whatever it takes. Just please, I'm begging, don't let either one of us kill someone." He paused, his throat closed off. He swallowed once, twice, three times. "I have a feeling if we do kill an innocent, the beast will destroy us both."

* * * * *

A bouquet of perfect long-stemmed roses arrived the next morning, and a truckload of contractors showed up at the front door a few hours later. They explained they'd been hired to complete the work in the kitchen.

Evidently Magus and Cyr could not or would not be finishing the job.

That evening, after the contractors left, Gina waited anxiously for a knock on the door. She wanted to know they were okay, but more than that, she needed to talk about what she saw last night. Somehow, she had to reconcile the monsters she saw tearing each other limb from limb with the gentle, patient lovers she knew.

Six o'clock, their usual time, came and went. Seven. Eight. Nine.

They weren't coming.

At ten, her grandmother handed her a book. "Read this." She gave her a kiss on the cheek and a pat on the shoulder. "I'm off to bed. Good night."

They truly weren't coming.

Book in hand, Gina prowled through the house, stopping at the living room window once every few minutes.

Were they okay?

She scowled at the romance novel, still clutched in her hand. She was so not in the mood for some sappy story at the moment.

Were they hurt? In jail?

Should she go next door and check?

She tossed the book on the coffee table and headed for the door. She'd just knock and if someone answered, she'd ask if they were hurt. That was all.

Nonono. She couldn't. Either Magus and Cyr didn't want to see her right now or couldn't. Whichever it was, she would look like an idiot going over there.

Shit. What if they were injured? Would they ask someone to let her know?

The man who'd walked her home had sounded so certain, though. He'd said the fight looked worse than it was. They were probably okay. Busy. Working. Or something. It wasn't like they'd promised to come over tonight.

Finally, having talked herself out of traipsing next door to check on her guys, she headed into the family room, sat down and flipped through the pages of her grandma's book. But she just stared at the print, not comprehending a single word. Every once in a while she'd glance at the roses, arranged in a pretty cut glass vase.

The flowers were so beautiful, each bloom absolutely perfect, such a stark contrast to the goofy vinyl thanksgiving tablecloth under it and cheesy 1970s plastic light fixture hanging above.

When it came to home décor, her grandmother paid little care to how things looked. Function trumped fashion every time. The woman's attitude was witnessed in every room of the house, from the bedroom Gina now called home, with its gaudy floral wallpaper, to the family room, featuring an outdated but comfortable brown and gold plaid sofa and mauve La-Z-Boy recliner. She supposed the house's out-of-date décor would pose a problem in the future. For now, it was as if time had stood still, and she was a college student again, enjoying a break from school. The house was exactly as it was then, even the smell.

Of course, that was all an illusion, everything had changed. She wasn't happy, at least not in the carefree way she'd been back then. Instead, worries about her grandmother, her own future, and thoughts of a couple of men weighed heavily on her shoulders.

If only she had someone to talk to.

Nostalgic, she set down the book, went to the hall closet and pulled down the box of old, faded photographs. Maybe a little trip into the past would help her deal with the present? Probably not, but since there was nothing on television and she simply could not focus on the book her grandma had given her, she was desperate for something to help her pass the time.

Hours dragged here, in this quiet place. Time moved slower than normal. Especially when it was late and she was lonely. But the photographs helped distract her, the images of a younger grandmother and grandfather—smiling, laughing, living—helped her racing thoughts slow, her body relax.

They looked so happy. In love. And she knew for a fact that they had been. Her grandmother still grieved the loss of her husband. They'd married when they were barely out of school, had lived together for fifty years, raising two daughters and facing life's uncertainties as one. Grandpa died only a few years ago, recent enough for Gina to remember how he'd held hands with her grandma when they'd walked into a grocery store, or how the two teased each other when they drove to their favorite restaurant on Sunday evenings.

If only she could have found that kind of love. The kind that endured decades. That strengthened the soul and fed the spirit.

It wasn't to be.

Tired, eyes blurred with tears, she packed away the pictures and went to bed. Her last thought as she drifted off to sleep was of her grandmother. Right now all they had was each other. Soon, though, Gina would lose her too. She sensed it in her gut. Then she would have nothing. No one.

Chapter Ten

ଧ

"You need to get out of this house," Gina's grandmother announced as she stirred her tea. She tapped her spoon against the cup like she always did, three times, tap, tap, tap, then set it on the paper plate that served as a saucer.

Gina handed her a piece of toast, wheat, extra butter. "I don't want to leave you home alone."

"I'm not a child. I don't need a babysitter."

Gina dropped a sliced bagel into the toaster and pushed down on the lever. "Of course you don't, but—"

Her grandma pulled the top off a small plastic package of grape jelly, stolen from the last restaurant they'd visited. She shook a butter knife at Gina. "You're young. You have your whole life ahead of you. You shouldn't be hiding away with me. Enough time has passed—"

"First, I'm not hiding. I don't know why you keep implying that." Gina opened the cream cheese and stabbed a knife into the center of the brick. "And second, I like it here."

Her grandma tsked as she spread some jelly on her toast. "You're right, it's gone beyond hiding now. You've burrowed so deep underground not even a mole would find you. But it's not solving your problems, is it? You're not happy."

"Yes I am." She intentionally ignored the other part of her grandmother's statement. "I'm extremely happy to be here with you. I love taking you out to your favorite restaurants and dance classes and even just sitting around watching slightly pornographic reality shows."

Her grandma stared down at her plate for several beats. "Young people need to spend time with people their own age."

"I don't mind spending all my time with you, Grandma. I swear, it hasn't been a sacrifice. I love you."

"You're a liar." Her grandmother took a bite of toast, chewed and swallowed. "I know the truth, so don't take me for a fool." She set down the toast and visibly sighed. "Please, Gina, it's Saturday." It was? Gina had completely lost track of the days. She glanced at the calendar hanging on the wall. "I insist you go out tonight. Do something with your friends. Maybe the boys next door will take you out."

Gina almost laughed at the suggestion. "I don't think so, Grandma." It had been several days since that night, the one she still couldn't erase from her memory. She'd tried. She'd watched all her favorite movies and read several of her favorite books. She'd worked into the wee hours of the night and then woken early in the morning to get back to work.

Thanks to all the hard work, her bank account wasn't looking quite so pathetic. That was a good thing.

"Then maybe you could find a nice show or maybe you could go dancing? I expect you to leave this house no later than eight and return no earlier than two."

"But Grandma, I have work—"

"I mean it, Gina. It's bad enough one of us is sitting here waiting for me to die—"

Gina dropped her bagel. "Oh Grandma, no! I'm not—"

"You've stopped living, and I let it happen. Dammit, if I could die tomorrow, just so you would finally give up the excuses and get back to living your life, I would. So go. Live life. You're young. Beautiful. And I love you too much to let you die with me." Her grandmother pushed back from the table. "If you refuse, I will be forced to do something I didn't want to do." She sighed wearily. "Don't make me sorry for letting you come and stay." After dropping that bomb, the angry woman shuffled out of the room, leaving Gina alone at the table, the remains of their breakfast cooling.

She dropped her face into her hands and just sat there. For seconds. Minutes. Hours? She had no idea how much time had passed. She heard nothing but the steady tick-tock of the cuckoo clock. Finally, when the clock marked the tenth hour with a series of metallic clangs and hollow cuckoos, she cleaned up the breakfast dishes.

Maybe her grandmother was semi-right—she was not waiting for the dear woman to die, nor was she hiding from anything or anyone. But she was losing herself. She wasn't participating in the real world anymore, just letting time trickle past, like the waters of the lazy creek that wound across the backyard.

Maybe she could go out for an hour or so. She hated movie theaters, so that was out. Dancing was fun, but she really didn't like going to a bar by herself. Dinner? Eat at a restaurant by herself? That didn't sound like fun either.

What would she be doing tonight if she hadn't moved in with her grandmother?

That was easy—what she did every Saturday.

Since she'd come to this small patch of rural heaven, she'd shackled the submissive in her. Perhaps that had caused some of the tension pulling her insides into knots. She hadn't left the compulsion that had led her to her first dungeon back in the city. It had followed her, like her shadow.

She wondered how far she'd have to drive to find a play party or bondage dungeon. Hours? That was out of the question. Yet, for kicks, she dialed onto the internet. A quick trip to a private forum she frequented produced the name of a dungeon within a half-hour drive. And thanks to a favorite Dom, she was the recipient of a personal invitation to check it out within hours. It seemed the wheels turning the world of Domination and submission turned fast when all the stars lined up and the fates were smiling upon a slightly desperate sub.

Her grandmother's mood lifted the instant Gina told her she would be going out that night. She dressed carefully, layering a conservative jacket and skirt over her latex dress. Her heart raced with giddy anticipation as she curled her long hair into perfect spirals and applied her makeup. After delivering a handful of warnings and a kiss to her grandmother, she carried her boots in a bag, wearing a pair of kitten-heel pumps out to her car.

As she drove, her twitchy nerves jangled and jumped. It had been such a long time since she'd played with a new Dom. She felt her palms dampening. It seemed she was more nervous now than her very first time.

By the time she pulled into the parking lot behind the building, a nondescript brick structure with no signs, her heart was thumping so heavily it felt bruised. Her hands were trembling slightly as adrenaline rushed through her system in wild, crashing waves. She felt slightly spinny-headed, intoxicated with anticipation. With care, she shrugged out of her normal-girl outer clothes, revealing a micro-mini latex dress underneath. She kicked off her kitten heels and slipped her feet into her boots. Now she was ready.

Or was she?

It had been months since she'd been to a dungeon. Her usual haunt was just a couple of miles from her apartment, an atmospheric place frequented by some of the area's most sought-after Doms. Above all else, she knew she was safe there. The Doms she had played with knew what they were doing and she could trust them implicitly. The one who had referred her to this dungeon, Master Anton, promised she'd find the same here. Tonight, he'd even arranged for her to meet a Dom he knew, Master Severo, owner of the dungeon, aptly named Wicked Garden.

She did a final makeup check then headed for the door, hands pressed against her outer thighs. She hurried across the parking lot and stepped into the lobby, which, like her home dungeon, looked a lot like the lobby of any business. A receptionist's desk sat directly in front of her, a glossy black counter curling around the good-looking receptionist sitting behind it.

Giving Gina a quick assessing glance, he hit a button on his headset, ending a phone call. "May I help you?"

Gina stepped up to the counter. "I'm here to see Master Severo. I have an appointment."

"Your name?"

"Gina."

"I'll let him know you're here. In the meantime, here are some documents we need you to look over." He handed her a clipboard, a pen clipped to the top and a small stack of papers held in place with the metal clamp.

"Thanks." Clipboard in hand, she sat in one of the sleek black chairs arranged around a low, round coffee table, a cozy waiting area.

The papers contained the usual disclaimers and rules. The last page was a long checklist, listing dozens of kinks and fetishes from which she could choose. She checked off the usual — bondage and immobilization, spanking, sensation play, psychological domination, body worship, anal training, role-play. Among submissives, she was on the light side, preferring psychological domination and mild sensation play over heavier pain play.

"Master Severo will see you now. His office is at the end of the hall." The receptionist motioned toward a doorway at the rear of the lobby. A metallic click suggested he'd remotely unlocked the door.

"Thank you." She hurried into the narrow hallway. She passed one, two, three, four sets of doors on each side of the corridor, each one bearing a brushed gold plate engraved with a name, Belladonna, Mandrake, Herbane, Jimsonweed, Hollowheart, Tailflower, Nightshade, Jessamine. The final door, situated on the far wall marking the end of the corridor, had no plate.

It opened into a room painted a deep burgundy color. The floor was covered in a pristine white carpet and two black leather couches sat along opposite walls. Above them hung large framed paintings of nude, bound women.

The room was empty, no Master Severo.

Knowing protocol from her other Masters, she stood in the center of the room, arms at her sides, waiting for his arrival. If things went as expected, today would be an interview, a discussion of her past experience, her expectations and perhaps plans for a future meeting.

Despite the energy buzzing through her body, she wasn't sure yet this was the right place, the right situation, for her. She was unsettled, her nerves snapping, as if tiny fingers were plucking them like guitar strings.

The door swung open behind her, and she twisted to look over her shoulder.

The air rushed from her lungs in a huff.

Magus tipped his head. "Hello, Gina."

"I...I...wow, this is a surprise." Her head was spinning.

Magus. The man she had been worrying about, thinking about, dreaming about for nights was here, in this place, interviewing her.

He was well. He wasn't injured. Those facts stirred up a batch of mixed emotions.

He was a Dom.

Why did that surprise her? She'd sensed his dominant nature. He hadn't needed to demand her submission to put her in her place. He'd done it naturally, with his voice, his touch, his body.

"Your Master, Anton, called in a referral." His expression, voice, body language gave no hint about what he was feeling. Not anger. Disappointment. Concern. Nothing.

"He didn't tell me—"

"He doesn't know."

"I see."

Magus circled her. "I thought perhaps you did, that you asked him for a referral so you could come see me." He lifted an index finger to her chin, and before she could respond, he added, "I don't think that any longer."

"I had no clue."

Something flashed in his eyes but in less than a heartbeat it was gone, making her question if it had been there in the first place. He dropped his hand, crossing his arms over his chest. "Why did you come here then?"

"I…"

"Do you regret your decision now?"

"No." Was that the truth? Honestly, she wasn't sure how she felt at the moment, except surprised, slightly off-balance, like the floor had rocked beneath her feet. He was standing there, so close and yet she felt as if there was a thick glass wall between them. He was so…impassive, detached.

"Answer my question."

"I came here because I was missing…something."

"And you thought an hour with Master Severo might be what you needed?" Still she saw, heard, sensed no sign of emotion. If only he would show her something, even anger was better than this, than nothing.

"Frankly, I wasn't sure. I was grasping. Things have been strange lately. Tense. I was looking for a release."

"I understand." He reached for her, setting his hand on her shoulder. It was far from an intimate touch. "Release?"

"Maybe that isn't the right word, the right thing."

114

His gaze sharpened for a fraction of a second. "Then what?"

"A connection?"

"With any man? Any Dom?" His voice was still completely emotionless.

"No. If Master Severo hadn't been you, I think I would've left without making an appointment to come back."

His lips curled into what might have been a smile, if there'd been any amusement in his face. "I'm not Master Severo."

"You're not?"

"No. He will be in shortly. I told him I wished to speak with you first."

Now she was more confused than ever.

"I am a Dom as well, but I declined Anton's offer."

"I see." She really, truly didn't, but she had to say something.

He stepped back from her and crossed his arms over his chest again. "For now I'm looking for something more significant from you than role playing...bondage games. I need something more real."

"*Real*," she echoed, even more confused than ever. What was he talking about? Everything she'd shared with Cyr and Magus had been nothing but real. Every touch, word, kiss.

Where were the shackles? The whips? The gags and blindfolds? The rules and expectations? Not once had any of those things been a part of their time together. Then again, she had been marveling about how he'd inspired her to submit without actually spelling it out. And there was that time when she'd called Magus "Master", assuming they were role playing, and they'd told her they weren't...

And then a little light flipped in her head, and she suddenly got it, why he'd been playing the games he had with her. He was trying to push her past the role-playing she hadn't even realized she forced on her lovers.

Playing Domination and submission games had become such an ingrained part of her intimate exchanges with men, she didn't realize she was playing them any longer.

"Which is it you want, Gina?" He circled her, stopping behind her. His hands slid down her sides, skimming over the snug material clinging to her hips. "Fantasy? Or reality?" He swept her hair over one shoulder and pressed his mouth to her nape. "Don't answer too quickly. Think." His breath tickled her skin, producing a tingly chill. "Fantasy is exactly what you imagine. Reality isn't always what you expect or want. With reality comes good and bad. Pleasure and pain. Joy and sorrow. Ecstasy and disappointment." His hands fell away, and he stepped back. Inside, she gave a silent whimper of disappointment.

More games?

Seduction was one tool this Dom wielded with skill. His every touch, word, expression stirred her emotions and ignited her desires. She wanted to drop to her knees and plead with him to allow her to serve him, but she sensed the minute she did that he would leave her.

"I don't know what to say, how to act."

"Follow your spirit, listen to your soul. It will guide you." He backed away, leaning against the door. "Should I tell Master Severo you're ready to meet with him?"

"No. I know now there was no way I could serve him. I have a Master already."

Magus shook his head, curled his fingers around the doorknob and twisted. "No, you don't. I told you, you can't be my submissive. Not yet. You don't trust me. I see it in your eyes."

Those words struck her hard, stinging like a physical blow, and she couldn't help reacting. She felt her teeth gritting, eyes narrowing. "I can't help being afraid, after what happened the other night..."

"There's a reason for what happened."

"Tell me."

"You're not ready to hear it yet." He left, the door closing behind him with a soft snick. She plopped on the couch and dropped her face into her hands.

As if things weren't confusing enough.

Chapter Eleven

ဆာ

Days passed without hearing a word from either Magus or Cyr. By the one-week mark, Gina was pretty sure she'd seen the last of her handsome pair.

It was so ironic, the fact that here she was a submissive, most definitely open to a new Dom, and the Dom she wanted didn't want her.

Crazy-making.

Gina went on as she had before she'd met Magus and Cyr. She cooked. She cleaned. She sewed and sewed and sewed. She drove her grandmother to doctor's appointments. She watched a lot of bad television and skimmed the pages of several romance novels. Morning, noon, evening, they blended into one dull blur. Time dragged.

Still, she reminded herself how precious these moments were. After another dose adjustment, her grandmother's Alzheimer's seemed to be well under control, her mind clearer than it had been in a long time. That meant no fires, and Gina could relax a little, not having to worry so much that her grandmother would hurt herself or wander outside and get lost. They spent their time debating the merits of certain reality television shows and comparing notes on books they'd read.

It was a quiet time, peaceful. Until one evening as she was heading in from a trip to the local library, she caught sight of Magus as he stumbled outside. The headlights of her car illuminated him and she saw his shirt torn to shreds, hair disheveled, face marred by deep welts.

Unable to do anything else, she jumped out of her car and ran to him, meeting him in his front yard. Up close, the red marks were even worse. "Magus! What happened?"

Instantly his expression changed. It was the most bizarre thing she'd ever seen, so shocking she literally lurched backward. Naturally, as she'd acted on impulse, she hadn't thought about the little wood border framing the flower bed behind her. Her ankle struck it, setting her off balance, and despite wind-milling arms, she became victim to gravity. Down she went, on her butt, smashing several petunia plants. Moist earth oozed into her shorts.

Without a word, Magus scooped her up and dropped her on her feet. She tipped her head to thank him and realized something other than his expression had changed.

The welts were gone. Vanished. Completely.

How?

Even if they'd been fake, there'd been no time for him to remove them.

What the hell?

"Your face?" She pointed.

"I'm fine," he said, stating the obvious.

"No, I see you're okay. Where did the marks go? They were deep, bleeding, terrible wounds. Nobody heals that quickly."

"Well, um…"

Before Magus had delivered a believable explanation—or any explanation for that matter—three men dashed out of the house behind her. Cyr led the pack, and like Magus, he looked semi-deranged, clothes ripped, hair mussed, face, neck and upper body marked with red scrapes.

He halted the moment his gaze found hers. And as she watched, her heart pounding faster with every second that passed, the red marks on his skin faded to pink then vanished completely.

"How?" was all she could manage to ask. Little pinpoints of light twinkled before her eyes.

Cyr rushed forward, face pulling into a mask of worry. "Gina?"

"I'm okay." Wobbly kneed, she shook her head, turned around and started back toward her grandmother's house. She hadn't seen what she thought. She couldn't have. It was…an illusion. Or something. The moonlight was playing tricks on her, the light cutting through tree branches and casting weird shadows on their skin. Maybe.

No, the moon was at their back. That couldn't be it.

She shut off her car, grabbed her purse and tote bag from the passenger seat and shuffled up to the porch. The second she reached it, she sat, welcoming the cool sensation of cement against her heated skin.

Magus and Cyr knelt before her.

"I've never seen anything like that before," she muttered, not really directing her comment to anyone in particular. All around her, the normal sounds, scents and sights of summer filled the world. Birds chirping. Soft wind teasing the leaves of the crabapple tree in her grandmother's yard, heavy gray clouds lazily drifting over the full moon, snuffing out the silvery light for a few seconds before wandering away.

It was a normal summer evening, and yet it wasn't. Normal couldn't describe what had just happened.

Again and again, she kept checking Cyr's and Magus' faces, shoulders, chests. Yes, those marks had been real. She simply didn't have that active an imagination. "How?"

"It's a little difficult to explain." Magus shifted to the side and sat next to Gina. Because the outside wall of the garage ran perpendicular to the porch, and he sat between the wall and Gina, he was close, too close.

"How would anyone explain the ability to miraculously heal?"

"Actually," Cyr said, glancing at Magus, "it's not hard to explain. It's just hard to believe."

She was even more confused than before. "Try me."

"Okay. It's simple. We heal quickly because we're immortal. We've lived for hundreds of years."

"I don't understand." Gina's mind raced. Thoughts whirled like leaves caught in a cyclone. "What do you mean, you're hundreds of years old? That's impossible."

"It is," Cyr agreed with a sober nod. "For the average man."

"You're not average," she echoed, agreeing with that statement, though not because she believed either Cyr or Magus was immortal.

"No," Magus said.

"You're immortal," she repeated.

This time, it was Cyr who responded, "Yes."

"Like, can't die?"

Magus nodded. "That's right."

Gina gave each guy a good, long look. "That's impossible. Only make-believe people, like romance novel and movie heroes, are immortal."

Magus' lips lifted into a crooked smile. "Romance heroes and guys like us."

"We'd like to think we could be romance novel heroes," Cyr added.

She didn't respond to that last comment. "I don't get this. Outside of some anger issues, you both seemed so...reasonable..."

Magus chuckled. "We're sane."

"Sane," she echoed, scooting backward. What was this? Why were they telling her this farfetched story now? What was the point? Surely not to scare her away. They hadn't come to see her, and she hadn't chased after them. She scrubbed her face, pulled her trembling hands from her cheeks and stared at her flattened palms. "I don't know what to say."

"Don't talk. Listen." Magus reached for her, but she felt herself flinch and he snapped his hand back as if he'd been stung. He stared down at the concrete sidewalk as he spoke, "It was many years ago. The dark spirits were threatening to destroy mankind. With every year that passed, more men fell under the enemy's spell. Wrath. Lust. Greed. Envy. Pride. Gluttony. Despair. Until the seven dark spirits ruled the world and all that was good was nearly wiped off the face of the earth.

"The gods were powerless against the enemy. Their spirits, Courage. Wisdom. Justice. Discipline. They could not defeat the spirits of sin. Nor could Honor. Humility. Obedience. Only the goddess' spirit, Mercy, had the strength to save all man. But the gods had to pay her price—a dear price it was too. They had to find fourteen men who were willing to sacrifice their mortality to save their brothers, fathers, sisters, mothers, children, grandchildren, great-great-grandchildren.

"Cyr and I are two of those men. Cursed. Blessed. Within us we carry a part of a dark spirit, Wrath. We are a vessel for the goddess. The other twelve possess the remaining six spirits. It was the only way to save the world. With the spirits contained, mankind was finally able to move out of the darkness."

Gina could only shake her head. Yes, she'd seen something she couldn't explain—injuries healed as if by magic. But this fairy tale, fantasy, whatever, stretched credibility to its breaking point. "This is too strange to believe."

Cyr placed his hand on top of hers. "Open your mind and let yourself believe. Remember, Gina. You saw us. Tonight. And a few nights ago. You know what you saw. The spirit of Wrath inhabits us, drives our desires."

"I did see you fight. But...spirits? It's like some kind of horror movie. *The Exorcist.* Though right now you don't seem angry. If you're possessed, why aren't you acting like it now?"

As if he sensed she was beginning to believe their explanation, Cyr curled his fingers around her hand and smiled. "That's because you quiet the spirit. You subdue it somehow. But once we leave you the spirit escapes and every time it is restrained and released, it destroys a part of our spirit, tainting our soul with its poison. We're losing ourselves. Losing the battle."

"You are our salvation," Magus stated solemnly.

"Me? Why?"

"The goddess has chosen you." Cyr released her hand and cupped her chin. The contact was too intimate right now, and his gaze, as it drilled into her eyes, unsettling.

"I don't understand." She jerked her head, wrenching her chin out of his hold. "I should go." Propelled by jitters, and the porch light flashing on and off, she pushed to her feet and grabbed her purse and bag. Twisting around, she stepped between the two men, climbing the one step to the porch.

Magus caught her ankle in his fist. By some miracle, she didn't fall on her face. He said, "You were chosen by the goddess. You are our blessing. Our virtue. Our miracle."

She kicked her foot, gently, but hard enough to let Magus knew she meant business. "I need to go. My grandmother is flipping the light."

"Okay." Magus visibly swallowed, something flashing in his eyes. Fear? Staring at her face, his expression dark, he released her ankle, one finger unfurling at a time.

Reluctantly and with a heavy heart, she pulled open the front door, stepped inside and pushed it shut.

No Grandma.

She peered through the peephole, knowing what she'd see. Sure enough, they stood there, side-by-side on the porch, the fading light emphasizing the dark shadows smudged beneath their eyes.

She spun around and leaned back. Her shoulder blades hit the door first, then her spine, head and butt. A few seconds later, after she'd wrung her trembling hands, she twisted around and checked the peephole again.

Still, they stood there, watching. They looked so sad. So lost and miserable. Haunted.

She shoved away from the door and headed toward the window. Even through the white sheer curtains, she could see they were still there. Unmoving. Silent. Ghosts.

She sank to the floor, the image of those faces burned into her memory, etched like a captured photograph onto film. Two dear faces. Two strong faces. Two faces full of soul-eating misery.

No, indeed. Magus had spoken the truth. He had no use for another submissive. No Master showed such desperate need to a sub. These men were suffering, being eaten up from the inside out by some dark evil. But did that mean they were what they said, immortal vessels of a goddess?

Gods. Goddesses. Sins inhabiting men. It was too strange to even imagine. To believe…impossible.

It had to be a story.

But what sort of truth could be at the root of this tale?

* * * * *

"Did you have a good time at the library, sweetheart?"

"Yes, Grandma. I did." Gina tugged on her mud-encrusted shorts self-consciously.

"Good." Her grandmother gave a satisfied nod. Patted the couch. "Come sit with me and show me the books you brought for us."

"Sure. Okay. But after I change. I had a little accident outside." Gina glanced at the clock on the microwave. "It's late. What are you still doing up?"

"I couldn't sleep. I've had a lot on my mind."

Gina sensed she wasn't going to like what she was about to hear. There hadn't been too many times when her grandmother had been the bearer of bad news. Every time she had, though, her voice deepened, her eyes darkened. "What is it, Grandma?"

"I feel it's time to make some changes."

Deciding she could change her clothes after, she stepped closer to her grandma. "What kind of changes?"

"I tried to avoid this, but you've given me no choice." Her grandma gave a weary sigh, as if it took every bit of strength she had to speak. "Someone wishes to lease the house."

"What? Grandma?"

"I told them they could move in immediately."

Stunned, Gina threw her hands over her mouth. It felt like everything was spinning around her. "Oh no. Why? Where will we live?"

Her grandma tugged a tissue from the box sitting on the table next to her chair. She dabbed her pale eyes, ringed with red as they teared. "The house is too much work. I can't manage the garden. It's being eaten by rabbits."

Garden? Gina dropped to her knees before her grandmother, placing her face in the direct path of her grandma's lowered gaze. "Oh Grandma, that's okay. We can buy our vegetables from the grocery store."

Her grandmother smiled, the expression not reaching her sad eyes, and patted her knee. "I'm tired. My hands don't work like they used to. My knees. I don't have the heart to spend my final days watching you work."

Gina placed her hand on top of her grandmother's, her smooth skin noticeably contrasting the heavily wrinkled, thin skin of her grandmother's. Straight, feminine, tapered fingers with neatly trimmed nails on top of bent, arthritic digits. "Your final days are a long way off."

"No, they're not. They're closer than you know. Right around the corner."

Gina didn't want to believe her grandmother. Did anyone know when they would go? No. "I'll fix this. When is this renter supposed to move in?"

"Like I said, immediately."

"But that doesn't give you any time to find someplace—"

"Already have."

"Oh?" Gina felt as if she'd been kicked in the gut. Stunned for the second time tonight, she fell back on her butt and stared up at her grandmother. She'd seen that look in her grandmother's eyes. More than once. "You've been planning this."

"Yes. It's been arranged for months. I wasn't ready until now though. It's time."

"Are you sure?"

"Absolutely. You'll take me?"

What choice did she have? If her grandmother had, indeed, made some kind of arrangements to rent the house, that was within her rights. She owned it. She could rent it to whomever she wanted. Immediately, Gina began speculating about where they would be moving. Maybe into some kind of apartment complex for elderly folks. That might be okay. "Sure, I guess..."

"It's for the best." Her grandmother settled her other hand on top of Gina's, gave it a soft pat. A second. "Good night, my sweet girl." Then she rocked forward, using the momentum to stand, and shuffled from the room.

"Good night." Tears blurring her vision, Gina watched her grandma, wondering what would happen next. It seemed everything was tumbling down around her ears. No, rather she felt as if she'd been hurled into space and was completely lost. Which way was up? Down?

When she finally had a grip on her emotions, she headed to bed.

When she woke the next morning, she found her grandmother in her bedroom, an ancient brown hard-sided suitcase sitting open on her bed. Already, she had it packed with folded garments. "Almost finished," her grandmother announced, standing in front of her dresser. The top drawer, the one that held all her jewelry, was open, a dozen or so cardboard jewelry boxes sat on the dresser's top. Her grandmother added another box to the stack.

"Right now? We're moving this morning?" Standing in the doorway, still wearing her pajamas and sporting bedhead, Gina shook her head. "Can't it wait until later this afternoon? I haven't had a chance to pack yet. Haven't taken a shower or cooked your breakfast—"

"I ate already. And there's no need for you to pack. I'm moving. You're staying here."

This made no sense. None at all.

A smidgen of hope flickered. What if this whole moving thing wasn't real? It could be her grandmother's medication again. When the dosage was off, it made her delusional. "I'm staying here? With the renter?"

"Yes." Her grandmother flipped the top of a small velvet box open and inspected the contents. "I can't leave this behind."

"But Grandma, if I stay here, how will you—"

"I'll be just fine." Her grandmother handed the velvet box to Gina then carried the rest of the boxes to the suitcase on her bed. "Please don't make this difficult." She arranged the boxes in the luggage then pushed the top of the suitcase over. "Could you please help me here? I never could get these latches."

Despite her confusion, Gina snapped the heavy case closed and dragged it off the bed.

Now what?

"I'm all set. But you're quite a sight. You should brush your hair and change your clothes before you take me."

Completely flabbergasted, Gina just stood there, in the middle of her grandma's bedroom, the heavy luggage at her feet. This was all so sudden and unexpected, she didn't know what to think. For weeks, her grandmother's behavior had been troublesome. She'd walked the halls at night, talking to her dead husband, wandered out of the house, mistaken Gina for at least a dozen other people, alternately acted like a lovesick teen and a depressed woman facing her final days of life. But lately—outside of a few little things—it had seemed her grandmother was getting better.

"Grandma, what year is it?"

"Two thousand eight. I am thinking completely clearly."

Gina didn't want to believe that, but she did. Kind of. Then her wishful thinking got the best of her and she decided this whole thing had to be a mistake.

A car ride might be just the thing to straighten out this mess. If her grandmother was confused, as she suspected, she would know it pretty quickly. There would be no destination.

Feeling slightly better, since this whole thing was probably nothing, she carried her grandmother's loaded suitcase out to the family room and set it down next to the door leading out to the attached garage.

"Go ahead and get cleaned up. Take your time. I still need to collect a few more things."

"Okay." Gina hauled the heavy bag out to the car in the garage and dumped it into the trunk. When she returned, her grandmother handed her a glossy folder with the words Silkwood Manor in gold, flourishing type on the front. Inside, she found a brochure from an assisted-living facility. And a receipt. Her grandmother had made a significant deposit to the facility months ago, several weeks before Gina had moved in with her.

Gina's heart dropped to her knees. "You don't have to do this. I came here to help you."

"And I appreciate all you've done, my dear, sweet girl. But I don't need you anymore. Someone else does."

"Someone else? Who?"

Her grandmother gave her a you-know-who look. "Do I need to spell their names out for you?"

Their? Plural. Gina's heart slammed against her rib cage. What had given her grandma such a crazy idea? She felt her jaw tighten, the stiff folder being crushed in her hands. "Did Magus and Cyr say something to you about me? Tell me, because if they did, I'll go over there right now and—"

"No, they didn't." Calmly, coolly, her grandmother tugged the folder out of her grip. "They didn't need to." She set it on the table, next to her purse.

"Then why, all of a sudden, are you so determined to leave? And why is it because of them?"

"It's not because of them. It's because the time is right. I told you that, dear. Now quit fussing and go get dressed so you can drive me to the home."

"But...it's only been a few weeks. I left my job, my life, to come here and help you—"

"No, you left your life to find a new one, which you have. If you won't drive me to the home, I'll call a taxi." With a don't-argue-with-me nod, she turned and headed back to her room to fetch whatever personal belongings she'd forgotten to put in her suitcase.

It seemed there was no chance of changing her grandma's mind. If there was one thing Gina knew about her grandmother, it was that once she'd made a decision, there was no chance of changing it.

Begrudgingly, Gina threw on a pair of jeans, pulled her hair into a messy ponytail and headed out to the garage. Already sitting in the car, her grandmother poked the button on the garage door's remote opener. The door rolled up, revealing a bright, sunshiny morning. The air smelled fresh, of grass and dew and earth.

Gina slid into the driver's seat and started the car. "Who is renting the house, Grandma?"

Her grandmother's smile was absolutely devious. "Magus and Cyr, of course. And don't you dare hold it against them. I asked them not to tell you because I felt it should come from me."

Chapter Twelve

ဢ

There was a familiar truck parked in the driveway when Gina returned to her grandmother's house a few hours later. Cyr and Magus' Explorer.

Her grandma hadn't been mistaken, no more than she'd been mistaken about the nursing home. Gina now had two new roommates, and there was nothing she could do about it, unless she either wanted to move into a place of her own or could convince Cyr and Magus to return to their house. With her limited income and virtually no savings, finding a place to rent wasn't going to be easy, but she had a feeling she wasn't going to be able to talk Cyr and Magus into giving up their new digs any easier.

She couldn't believe they'd known about this all along and hadn't even hinted at it.

Feeling like a pawn in a chess match, Gina shut off the car and went in the house. The family room, living room and kitchen were empty. No sign of the guys. Desperate to beg them to put off their move—at least for a few weeks, until she could figure out where she could go—she searched the rest of the house. That was the least they could do for her, considering everything.

Blech, she felt woozy. Adrenaline was making her nerves twitchy, and she knew her jitters wouldn't ease until after the confrontation was over. Better to get it over right away.

Hands wringing, she wandered back to her grandmother's bedroom first. The door was ajar. "Cyr? Magus?" When no one answered, she pushed it open. "Oh!"

The furniture was different. In the place of her grandma's red velvet-covered headboard, stood an enormous floor-to-ceiling wood headboard. But that wasn't what she noticed first. It was Magus, lying spread-eagled on the bed, wrists and ankles wrapped in metal shackles, and heavy chains securing them to the head and footboards.

"Oh God. I'm sorry." Shock finally registering in her slow-as-molasses brain, she spun around and hurried out of the room, slamming the door behind her. "Magus was chained to the bed," she jabbered to nobody. "I can't believe I barged in on him like that." Her cheeks were burning so hot, she wondered if they might blister.

Clearly, the conversation she had planned would have to wait.

She raced into her room and shut the door, falling back against it. The smooth wood felt cool against her burning back. "I can't believe I did that." She let her head fall forward and covered her sizzling face with her hands. A bizarre giggle-whimper slipped up her throat. It seemed every time she turned, something more bizarre was waiting for her. Freakish stories about immortal men. A grandmother who preferred to be locked up in a nursing home than live with a granddaughter who loved her. Now this.

What was next?

"Gina." Magus.

She threw her head up. The back struck the door. *Thunk.*

"It's okay, Gina. Come here," he called.

Okay? Her cheeks cooled a smidge.

When she returned to his room, Magus gave her a smile that seemed so out of place, considering his current situation. He shook his arms. "The chains are for safety. I'm okay as long as you're home. You can unlock me."

Safety?

A few questions leapt to her mind but she didn't say a word, other than to ask where the key for the heavy padlocks had been stored. Once she had freed Magus, he led her to Cyr, chained in what had once been her grandfather's bedroom.

That wasn't her grandfather's room anymore.

The house wasn't her grandma's.

Everything was different. Everything.

Once she had both men released, she followed them into the family room and, at their suggestion, sat down. Her stomach felt strange. A little woozy. And her head felt funny too, like everything inside her skull was churning.

"You're pale." Cyr headed to the kitchen. "Maybe a glass of water will help."

Magus stood in front of her, his mouth pulled into a thin line. "This is a lot for you to handle all at once. Are you okay?"

Cyr handed her a glass of ice water.

She thanked him and then returned her attention to Magus. Her eyes were burning. Her nose too. She concentrated on breathing slowly. In. Out. Innn. Outttt. She lifted her hands to her face. Her fingers were trembling. She pressed them to her lips. "I...don't know what to say. I don't think it's right for me to stay here with you. It's your house now. I'll get in the way." She blinked once, twice, three times. "Why didn't you tell me?"

The guys exchanged a tense look.

Cyr pulled a chair from the dinette and set it next to Magus then he went for a second one. They each sat.

Cyr leaned forward, his elbows propped on his knees. "You are more than welcome to stay here. That's always been the plan."

She blotted her blurry eyes with her sleeve. "I can't believe you didn't tell me." The woozy feeling was getting worse. She hiccupped.

Cyr's expression darkened. "Isobel made us promise. We didn't want to keep any secrets from you, but we agreed your grandmother should be the one to tell you."

"We want you to stay."

Swallowing a sob, she looked at Cyr then Magus then Cyr again. "I don't know. I feel like I don't belong here anymore."

"You own the house," Magus stated.

She fingered her damp sleeve. "No, it's my grandmother's house. Even if I did, that would technically make me your landlord. How many landlords live with their tenants?"

Magus shrugged. "We don't care about technicalities. Never have."

Cyr captured her attention by lightly flicking his fingertips over hers. "Your grandmother made us promise you would be welcome to stay."

Made us promise. That didn't make her feel any better. In fact, that sent another sob tearing up her throat. She held her breath to keep it from slipping out. "Another promise?" she asked.

"That's not to say," Magus added, as if he could read her thoughts, "we don't want you here. We do want you to stay. More than you realize. What do you want?"

She let out the huge lungful of air she'd been holding. "Honestly, I don't know. Why would you want me hanging around? You're both single men." *Men with certain needs, the kind you don't want me sating.* She clenched her hands together and dug her nails into the skin. "Wouldn't you rather have your privacy?"

There was no way she could stay here, knowing they would be bringing other people...would be intimate with other... *No. Just no.*

"We want you here because..." Cyr slid Magus a quick glance. "I wouldn't want to stay here without you." This time it was Cyr who sighed. "I'm no good at talking about this stuff. I always say the wrong thing."

Tears spilling from her eyes now, Gina shook her head. "You're better at it than the last guy I dated."

Beside Cyr, Magus stiffened a little at her comment.

Taking a cue from Magus' body language, she asked, "What about you, Magus? If you tell me you want me to leave I will. No hard feelings."

He didn't hesitate, "Hell no, I don't want you to leave."

Even though he'd answered so quickly, she didn't believe him. She wanted to. Desperately. "I sense you aren't happy about something."

Magus' eyes jerked to the side. "It has nothing to do with the house."

She shifted, putting herself smack dab in the center of his field of vision. "Are you sure?" Why wouldn't he tell her the truth? *He's trying to spare my feelings.*

"Yes." His dark expression belied his words.

Liar. *Just fucking say the words. Please. You want me to leave. I know.* "What's wrong?"

"Nothing, if you tell us you'll stay," Cyr answered for him.

"No." Magus backhanded Cyr's shoulder. "She knows she's welcome. We aren't going to pressure her." Then he turned to her. "If you want to leave, Gina, then go. You've sacrificed enough."

Then go.

His words were like a punch in the gut. No—worse, a kick. He didn't want her there because he wanted his freedom. She would get in the way, just like she'd said. He only offered to let her stay out of a sense of obligation, a promise.

Oh God, she felt sick. She needed to get out of there. Leave. Today. Now.

Cyr gave Magus a bewildered stare. "But you know what'll happen. We should tell her."

"What'll happen if what, Magus? If I leave or if I stay?"

Magus shook his head, forcing what she guessed was supposed to be a carefree smile to his face. "Don't worry about that. It's no big deal."

135

"Cyr?"

"If you leave, the spirit will destroy us. Our souls," Cyr answered. "We need you."

Cyr's response was like another kick in the belly. These men didn't want her, they didn't care for her, they didn't want to build a relationship with her. No, they believed they *needed* her. No wonder Magus had said he didn't want her submission. When he'd said he wanted something more real, he hadn't meant he wanted affection, love, commitment. He wanted her...what? How did he expect her to save them?

"How am I supposed to save you?" she asked. "What do you need from me?"

"Just be close by. When you're in the room with us, the spirit is subdued," Cyr answered.

So that was it? They believed she needed to sit in the same room with them to cure them? Nothing more? The knot in her gut pulled tighter.

Trying to hide how awful she felt inside, she looked straight into Magus' eyes. "Magus, why would you keep something that important from me? First, the thing with the house, and now this. It makes me wonder what other secrets you're hiding."

"I've never kept anything secret that might hurt you," Magus stated, sounding genuinely convinced. He was totally deluded if he believed his secrets hadn't hurt her, but she figured it was pointless telling him that if he couldn't figure it out for himself. "If you need to go, then go. Don't worry about us."

There. That was as close as he was getting to saying *I don't want you here*. She could leave now.

It was the best thing for all of them. Yes, the best.

Unless they were telling the truth about the spirit thing.

No, they couldn't be. Spirits?

What if they were?

She looked at Cyr. He'd said they needed her, and clearly he believed it. She could see the desperation in his eyes, on his face.

Need wasn't wanting or liking or loving. Then again, she'd made it crystal clear that she wasn't ready for a serious relationship. She had plans, a life to go back to. That was what she wanted. Wasn't it?

She dropped her head, covering her face with her hands. This was so confusing. How could she sort it all out?

First, could she believe their claims about the spirit?

She'd seen their miraculous healing, and she couldn't deny something beyond ordinary was going on. Cyr and Magus were not your average men. Out-of-this world looks and bodies aside, they were special, in so many ways. They were kind, sweet, attentive, generous. Special in all the ways a woman would want a man to be. And then some. That was no doubt why she was so hurt by their lies. So devastated by their rejection. And so torn about whether to leave or not.

Injuries that should take weeks to heal mended within seconds. They couldn't be totally human. And if she could believe that much, she could also believe they might be destroyed by whatever spirit or demon or whatever was responsible for the miraculous healing she had witnessed.

The answer was yes, she could believe them. Which meant they did need her.

Second, where did that leave her? Living with two men she was attracted to…she cared about…she longed for…and watching them take other lovers. It would be her sacrifice to make, her price to pay so they wouldn't be killed by the evil spirit inside them.

How long could she live like that? Would the longing ease eventually? Would the heartache slowly eat away at her soul or would it diminish as weeks and months passed?

It didn't matter.

She couldn't leave. She didn't want anything bad to happen to either man. They didn't deserve to suffer. She cared. A lot. Enough that it made her sick to think of them dying. Especially if she could do something about it. How selfish would it be to pretend nothing horrible would happen and go on her merry way?

"You *need* me to stay then." Outside of her grandma, nobody had ever needed her. Not like this. Not so desperately.

Cyr nodded. "Yes. But I agree with Magus. If you feel you must leave, then I want you to. I just felt you should know the truth before you made a decision."

"You're manipulating her," Magus practically growled.

Cyr shot Magus a scowl. "No, I'm not manipulating her. Just the opposite, I'm letting her make an informed decision, based on all the information. You would rather let her make one based on half the facts? What if she left and later learned what the consequences were? Don't you think that would hurt her, if not destroy her? Guilt is a sharp blade. It can cripple the strongest person."

At Cyr's emotion-filled words, Gina pushed to her feet. Her emotions were all over the place. Sadness. Elation. Confusion. Worry. Guilt. "I need to think. I'm overwhelmed. So many changes." She gave each one a silent apology. "I need to be alone for a little while, to think some things through. But I'll be back."

Magus made a shooing motion with his hand. "We'll call Amun. He'll take care of us. Go."

Insides churning, she headed out to the car. As she started it, Amun jogged across the front yard. He disappeared into the house before she had backed down the driveway.

With absolutely no clue where she was headed, she drove. Down country roads lined with miles and miles of corn fields. Her thoughts whirred through her mind as she drove. Memories of moments shared with Cyr and Magus, both sweet and sad. The out-of-control emotions only got worse as she found her way onto the freeway. Trees whizzed past in a blur of green. Miles whirred past in a blur of gray. Time flew past in a blur of empty, lonely confusion.

She'd seen all the proof she needed. Magus and Cyr were not human. They would live forever. They healed magically. And she cared about them, really, truly cared. How would she leave? How could she say goodbye? They needed her, desperately, just like her grandmother had said.

Her grandmother had known about them. How?

Grandma, you are so devious.

At the first exit ramp, she headed back, a destination finally decided upon—a certain nursing home, housing an elderly woman who, when she thought about it, had to have been plotting and scheming all along.

Had her grandmother asked her to move in just so she could play cupid? The pain she had unknowingly caused for Cyr and Magus.

When she walked into her grandmother's room at the home, she had a speech all ready. But her grandmother was nowhere to be seen. Not in her room. Or in the adjoining bathroom. As Gina exited the bathroom, a beautiful young woman turned the corner from the hallway, freezing, picture-perfect mouth shaped into a little O of surprise, wide-set eyes bugging.

"Wrong room. Sorry." The woman wheeled around and rushed back out into the hallway.

That face...

Gina stood in her grandma's dark, empty room, staring at the open door. She'd seen that woman somewhere before. Where?

Nagging curiosity propelled her forward, toward the hall, but all she found was an empty corridor, with the exception of one person, her grandmother, snoozing in a wheelchair, parked in front of the nurse's station. The woman was gone. And forgotten.

"There you are." Gina shuffled down, retrieved the chair and wheeled her snoring grandmother back to her room, parking it next to the bed.

Now what? As riled up as she was about what she suspected her grandmother had done, she didn't have the heart to wake her. Uncertain, she sat on the bed, plunked her elbows on her knees and dropped her chin in her hands.

All those lines, mapping her grandmother's face. She tried to visualize her grandma as a young woman, at her age, as she'd been in those smudgy old black and white photographs Gina couldn't seem to stop looking at.

Her grandma's eyelids fluttered and lifted. "Gina? What are you doing here?"

"I came to see you, Grandma. I told you I would."

"Yes, but you just left." Her grandmother headed for the mini-fridge in the room's corner. "Do you want a cola?"

"No thanks. I need to ask you something."

"Oh? You couldn't have called?" A can of Pepsi in her hand, her grandmother settled into the recliner next to the refrigerator. She started working at the pull tab on the can, a nearly impossible task with her arthritic fingers.

"Let me get that." Gina opened the can and handed it back to her grandma. "I wanted to talk face-to-face."

"Okay." Her grandmother snatched up the small brown bag sitting on top of the refrigerator. "Cookie?" She chomped into what looked like a peanut butter cookie.

"No thanks. Why didn't you move in here months ago, when you first paid your deposit?"

Her grandmother washed down the mouthful she'd been chewing with a swig of her soda. "Because I wasn't scheduled to move in until right around the time you moved in. And I didn't have the heart to leave right after you arrived."

"I understand, but why not tell me your plans before I moved? I could've taken a leave from work and stayed with you for a few weeks, instead of quitting my job."

Her grandmother shook the cookie at her, filling the air between them with the scent of peanuts. "You wouldn't have done that."

"What makes you say that?"

"Because I never asked you to leave your job and stay with me in the first place. That was your idea. You wanted to come so I let you."

Gina watched her grandma polish off the rest of the cookie then help herself to a second one. "Okay, I'll give you that. You didn't ask in so many words, but you — "

"No, no. Don't you think it's time to quit lying? Look in the mirror, Gina. Ask yourself why you were so eager to run away from your life."

"I wasn't running away from anything. What was there to run from? A great job. A nice apartment. Friends."

"You don't need me to answer that question, dear. You know."

Searching for a way to steer the conversation back on track, Gina watched her grandma eat yet another cookie before voicing her suspicion plainly, "I think you planned this all along."

"Planned what?"

"For Magus and Cyr to move into the house."

"Yes, I did. We talked about it awhile back, before I signed the contract with this place."

"No, I mean for them to move into the house with me."

"Oh dear, I couldn't have planned for that. How could I possibly know you would be quitting your 'great job' in the city, and leave your 'nice apartment' and all your friends behind? Let alone how would I have known you'd get along with those boys so grandly?"

"Exactly. How would you know?"

"I couldn't."

"But you did."

"No, dear."

Just then, that young woman's face flashed through her mind, and Gina remembered where she'd seen it before. "Grandma, there was a lady here, in your room. I remember her from the dance studio. Is she a friend of yours?"

"I don't know who you're talking about. I didn't know anyone at the studio. I'd never been there before. How could I?" After a beat, her grandma asked, "What are you going to do?"

"About what?"

"The house." Her grandmother brushed the crumbs off the front of her shirt. "It's yours. I signed the Quit Claim Deed this afternoon. The lawyer will be bringing papers for you to sign in the next few days."

"You did?"

"I'd already promised the boys they could rent it, but only for six months. I didn't have the heart to tell them they couldn't have the house after they'd waited so long. I hope you'll let them stay. There are six boys living next door. It's become terribly crowded. They offered to buy the house, but I refused to sell it to them. Anyway, since you needed some time to find a new job, I thought you could use the help. They are paying a lot of money for the rent, and every penny is yours, to use as you need. I put the first month's payment into the joint account."

"Then you haven't been trying to play cupid?"

"No." Her grandmother's gaze dropped to her hands, clasped in her lap. "Okay, maybe I was doing a little matchmaking when I wandered over to their house that night. I wasn't expecting you to fall in love, just come to know each other a little. I thought that might make the living arrangements more comfortable later." Her grandmother wrung her hands. "I hope you won't go back to the city. I'll never see you. You're all I have."

No pressure there. "I couldn't leave you, Grandma. You know that."

"Then you'll stay with the boys?"

"Yes."

Briefly, she thought about asking her grandmother if she knew about their unusual qualities, but even thinking about saying such things aloud made her feel silly. Overall, her grandmother's explanation was logical, believable. There was no reason to think she knew any more about Magus and Cyr, other than their wish to find a new home.

Still, one question remained. Why would two professional athletes, who had to make millions of dollars a year, rent a house when they could easily afford to buy any house they wanted?

Chapter Thirteen

ↇ

The house was quiet when Gina returned. She headed back toward the bedrooms, expecting to find her new roommates tied to their beds like they had been earlier.

Magus wasn't.

Neither was Cyr.

Both rooms were ransacked, furniture overturned, the contents of drawers and closets strewn all over the floor.

"Shit. What happened? Magus! Cyr!" Her heart thumping heavily in her chest, she raced through the house, calling their names. After searching every inch, from the basement to the garage, she dropped onto the couch and flopped her head back. Blindly, she stared up at the ceiling. That lasted about five seconds then, spurred on by gut-wrenching worry, she ran next door and rang the bell.

"Gina." Amun opened the door wider, stepping aside to let her inside.

Gulping air frantically, she pointed toward her grandmother's house. "They're gone. I just got home. Their rooms are a mess."

"It's okay." He set a soothing hand on her shoulder. "They're here."

"Oh thank God." The tension in her body literally slid down her legs.

He smiled and motioned toward the back of the house. "I'll go tell them you're home."

"Okay."

She stood in the living room, hands clutched, watching Amun round a railing that framed a set of stairs leading to the family room area below. When he didn't return a few minutes later, she wandered toward the staircase, shuffled down the steps, quietly, and halted at the bottom. Nobody was in the family room, but she heard voices coming from the door on the opposite side of the landing.

The door was slightly ajar.

She knew it was wrong to peek.

Rude.

She did it anyway.

It was a bondage dungeon, a pretty well-stocked one from the look of it. Well populated too. Men and women were making use of the many kneelers, benches, tables and chairs scattered around the room. After a few seconds of searching she found Cyr standing in front of a metal cage. Magus was next to the wall, staring down at a woman kneeling before him. She was nude.

A pang of jealousy burned through Gina's body, and she bit her lip against the temptation to blurt out a mouthful of expletives.

A woman was kneeling before Magus, the Dom who had rejected her. And who was that with Cyr? A woman. No, two women.

Oh God, how was she going to deal with this?

She swallowed hard. Three times. She had no right to tell them who to play with. They had made no commitments to her. Her brain knew that. The rest of her, particularly her heart, seemed to be having a hard time accepting the cold, hard facts.

She jerked back, catching some movement in her peripheral vision as she hauled ass toward the sliding glass doors at the opposite end of the family room. The contents of the room passed her in a blur. Just a few more steps and she would be outside, could breathe again.

She twisted the door's lever, pulled it open, stumbled outside. The sun was hovering low over the western horizon, the sky cloudless, the air heavy with the scents of sun-toasted earth. It was a pretty evening. The kind that should have lifted her spirits. Nothing would do that now. Everything was so messed up.

"Gina."

She stopped in her tracks. By God, she wanted to keep going, to stomp her way home, slam the door and lose herself in a quart of ice cream and some really bad reality TV. What she didn't want to do was stay there and listen to some ridiculous explanation for something she shouldn't be upset about.

Regardless, she didn't walk away. She stayed right where she was, although she didn't look at Magus. Instead, she focused on the ground.

"Why did you come here?" He was close. Near enough that the slight edge in his voice sent a shiver down her back.

"I was worried about you." *You jerk.*

"I appreciate that. But did Amun invite you downstairs?"

"No. And I admit, that was rude." She toed a rock. "I guess I deserved to see what I did."

"What did you see?" When she didn't answer right away, he gave her shoulder a light tap. "Gina, tell me."

"I saw you, playing with some woman."

"Is that truly what you saw?"

"There was a female kneeling at your feet."

"Does that mean I was playing with her?"

"I suppose not."

He moved closer. His breath warmed her nape. "I told you, I'm not looking for a submissive."

"Which means you have one," she said between teeth that were irritatingly gritted. "So I assumed she was it—the *chosen one.*"

"Such fury. You're jealous."

She shrugged. It was too obvious to deny.

"Tell me, Gina, would you rather submit to me or be my partner?"

"Partner? Or savior?" she snapped.

"Partner." He gripped her upper arms, giving them a gentle squeeze. "I never said I wanted you to stay to save me. If you're sticking around because you think I'll die, then I want you to go. No, I demand you to go."

"I can't, dammit." She took a single step away from him and dug her fingers into her hair, scraping her fingernails over her scalp. "Not if you'll die. Will you?"

"I can't say for sure. I might not. I thought you didn't believe what we told you about Wrath. You accused me of lying."

"And you didn't deny it."

"Why would you want to give yourself to men who lie to you?"

Good point.

"Actually, I don't think you're *lying*-lying. Keeping secrets, yes. And I do believe what you told me about the spirit. I guess I have from the beginning. I just had a hard time accepting my belief, if that makes any sense."

"Not really."

Of course, he'd said that. He wasn't going to let her get away with a half-assed confession. He was going to make her admit everything, say what she hadn't been able to before. "I didn't want to admit to myself that I believed you were possessed by a supernatural being. Even though I couldn't deny what I'd seen."

"Why?" He circled her, stopping directly in front of her.

Slowly, she lifted her gaze. Up his legs, his stomach, chest, to his face. That beautiful face. "I guess I have a hard time believing anything, even what I see."

One eyebrow quirked. That side of his mouth lifted too. "Such a revelation you've had. In a very short time."

"That's one thing I will say about myself." She crossed her arms over her chest and let her weight shift to one hip. "I don't take long to make progress. And even if I do try to deny reality, I can't keep it up for long."

He tweaked her nose. From any other man, that gesture would have made her furious. But not Magus. "How is your grandmother feeling about her new living arrangements?"

"She seems happy."

"Very good."

She pointed at the house they now shared. "Do I want to ask what happened after I left?"

He grimaced. "Probably not."

"But you're okay?"

"I am now. I can't speak for Cyr though. He's still inside, and Wrath is probably tearing him up. He spent the better part of the time you were gone locked in that dog cage.

"Should we check on him?"

"That's a good idea." He cupped her elbow in his hand, gently leading her back into the house, across the family room and into the dungeon. The people around her — with the exception of one — were too involved in what they were doing to even notice someone new had walked into the room. It didn't matter. The only one who she cared to notice did, the second her toe crossed the threshold.

He was back in the cage, his face a mask of pain, fading red marks marring his bare chest and arms. The women who had once been with him were now standing a safe distance away and talking to each other with tipped heads and low voices.

When Magus stepped up to them, they turned. "This is Gina," he said.

Both women immediately fell to their knees, assuming the position Gina was all too familiar with. Were they expecting to play with Magus now, while she was watching? Was that what typically happened in this place?

She couldn't watch Magus play with another submissive. No way. Even if it was just playing, not real.

Real...

She met Cyr's gaze.

"Gina. My salvation." Cyr's lips curled up and the second Magus had the cage door open, he grabbed her by the waist, hauled her against him and kissed her.

It was the most decadent, heavenly kiss, full of raw emotion. Stirred by desperate longing, she returned the kiss, unleashing all the sadness, confusion, wanting and desire she'd pent up the past few days.

Stroke by stroke, nip by nip, genuine, overwhelming emotion poured out of her. She curled her fingers into his hair and clawed at his shoulder with the other hand. Tears burned her eyes, seeping from the corners as sobs quaked up her throat and filled their joined mouths.

Behind her, Magus gathered her hair over one shoulder and kissed her nape. Instantly, her upper body was coated in goose bumps. Prickly tickles buzzed along her nerves, making her shudder. When Cyr broke the kiss, she let her head fall to the side, and Magus took full advantage of her exposed neck, kissing, licking and biting a path up to her ear.

She felt like she was being swept up in a churning tide of heat. All around her, sounds of ecstasy blended into a symphony of need. Voices, male and female. Sighs, moans, cries of ecstasy. The snap of a whip. The clank of a chain. The sloughing whisk of skin gliding over skin.

Her eyes were closed yet she saw images of writhing bodies, nude, giving and receiving every kind of carnal pleasure. The sight, coupled with Magus' and Cyr's kisses and strokes, made her legs go soft. Strong arms swept her off her feet and carried her effortlessly across the room. She opened her eyes to find it was Cyr who carried her. He was taking her out of the dungeon, away from the others. Through the family room.

Magus followed. His need was visible, in every line on his face, the set of his jaw and the flame flickering in his eyes. Tonight, he would not stop. She knew it and she was glad. Gina was so overjoyed, more tears gathered in her eyes.

It was as if something had snapped in her brain, a switch, and now it was so clear. She'd been using the bondage games as a barrier. With all the rules and expectations, roles and fantasy scenarios, it was so easy to be safe. To guard her heart.

Out they went. The western sky was lavender, deep purple and brilliant salmon, the colors darkening toward the east. Twilight.

Cyr walked around the back of their former home, turning toward the sloping rear of the backyard. Toward the towering lilac bushes. Tiny purple petals coated the grass, in the dim light looking like fat, grape-hued snowflakes. He dropped to one knee and set her down on them and she inhaled, drawing in the glorious scent of the flowers.

This place had always been special. Framed by the flowering shrubs, it was like a secret garden. Her secret garden. What better place for this moment, with these men, than here?

"Make love to me," she pleaded, reaching for her shirt. "Here. Now. Both of you. Please. I understand why you wouldn't play submission games now. I really do. You wouldn't let me hide. It wasn't enough for me to give you my body. You wanted my heart too."

Magus dropped to his knees beside her and took her hand in his. Sweetly, he kissed each fingertip on both hands. One at a time, his eyes boring into hers. When he reached her pinky, he let them fall and cupped her face. "Tell me, what is your most beautiful part?"

She found the answer in his eyes. No guessing this time. The word whispered through her mind. "My heart."

"You are the joy our Wrath cannot eclipse. You are the light no dark spirit can conquer." He placed her hands on his chest. "You are the master of my soul. And the slave of my heart."

Those were the most beautiful words she had ever heard. This was the most beautiful moment she had ever shared with anyone.

Speechless, she swallowed a sob and cupped her hands over her mouth. What could she possibly say after that?

Gently, he pulled her hands from her face and placed them on his chest again. "Do you feel that?" His voice was hoarse.

"What?"

"I think the spirit is weeping." He turned to Cyr. "Do you feel it?"

"Yes, Magus. Yes I do." They clasped hands and exchanged teary smiles. "What does it mean? Has it been defeated? Are we complete?"

"I don't know. I don't think so. Not yet." Excitedly, he pushed her hands down toward his pants' fly. "Undress me, Gina. Undress us. Serve us. And let us serve you. Something wonderful is happening."

"More wonderful than me falling in love with you?" she whispered.

"Nothing is more wonderful than that." Cyr looked at her with eyes full of rapture as he removed her shirt.

Gina stood to give herself better access to the guys. After unzipping Magus' pants, she pushed them down over his narrow hips. He dropped onto his butt to let her tug them down his lean, muscular legs. A minute later, she had his underwear off as well and he was kneeling in the moonlight, the moon's rays reflecting silver off his gleaming skin, making him look like a marble statue formed by the hand of the most talented artist of all time. Beautiful.

Cyr removed all her clothes before she was allowed to take off his. It didn't take long before all three were there in the grass, on bent knees, touching, kissing and stroking every exposed inch of each other's bodies. Each served the needs of the others, touched where they craved to be touched. Held as they hungered to be held. Kissed when they longed to be kissed. Three bodies coming together as one. Three minds working as one. Three souls joining as one.

Magus rolled on a condom and sat down, pulling Gina onto his lap, holding her by the waist. Legs straddling Magus' hips, arms draped over his shoulders, she impaled herself on his shaft. Finally. Oh yes, finally. She'd waited so long for this. He'd made her wait. But now she was grateful.

She held him deep within her now. Rocking her hips back and forth, she ground her pussy into his groin. *Yes, good. But it would be better if...* "Cyr?" she whispered.

"I'm here," he murmured, kissing the back of her neck.

"I need you too. Both of you." She lifted herself then swiftly dropped back down. The friction inside made her shudder and Magus groan. "Take me. Claim me. Make me yours."

"Lube?"

"I grabbed some as we were leaving," Magus rumbled. "Pants pocket."

"You are brilliant." She rewarded him with a kiss.

He, in turn, rewarded her with a kiss back.

While Cyr found the lube, Magus positioned them both so Cyr could access her ass.

With dampened fingers, he tested her hole, slowly stretching it. Absolute ecstasy.

She whimpered into Magus' mouth and tightened her back, arching her spine to allow Cyr easier access to her hole. "Oh yes, Cyr. Please."

"I can't not take you now."

That was a promise. One that made her shudder with need.

She relaxed the muscles as his cock pressed against them, and in it slipped. Such a glorious feeling. Magus supported her with his arms, lifting her off him so he could surge his hips forward and thrust inside. As his cock glided in and out of her hungry pussy, Cyr's slowly worked itself deeper in her anus. Filling, stretching, claiming her. Finally he stilled, his cock pushed as deep as it could go.

"Touch her clit," Cyr said, his voice a breathy rasp. "I need to feel her come."

"Can't," Magus shifted his hold on her but he didn't release her.

"I can." She reached down and fingered the tight bud, and with the first touch, a blade of heat licked up her spine.

"More, Gina. Come for us." It was a command, spoken by one of the masters of her heart, soul and body.

She stroked herself again, and againagainagain. Back and forth, softly at first. The guys took their pleasure, thick cocks penetrating her, the friction gliding along her nerves, sizzling up and down her spine. Delicious heat pounded in throbbing pulses through her body. Out from her center it rushed, in waves that zapped like surges of electrical charges. Up her neck to her scalp. Down to the soles of her feet.

Magus cupped her breasts, pinched her nipples, and she cried out into the silent night, desperate for the release that was building with every heartbeat, every touch, every thrust of those two glorious rods.

Faster she stroked, and faster they invaded her. Twin shafts driving in and out of her body, stroking where she needed it most, filling her to the point of almost agonizing ecstasy.

So close. Right there.

Her feet tightened. Legs. Stomach. Chest.

Yes, oh yes.

"Come now, Gina," Magus demanded.

Her orgasm slammed through her like a tidal wave crashing through a dam, unleashing a torrent of bliss so powerful, she dropped forward, bones turned to jelly. Her pussy and ass cyclically squeezed and relaxed around Cyr's and Magus' cocks as they pounded in and out. Beneath her, Magus' skin was coated in a slick sheen, his muscles trembling beneath his glimmering skin. Behind her, Cyr growled then surged forward, and the orgasm that hadn't faded amplified again, a second release. Her cries echoed off the trees as a soft, sweet breeze swept over her burning skin.

Magus' fingers dug into her hips as he ground his groin into hers. He too growled when orgasm gripped him. His thrusts grew jerky and fast as he rode the waves of ecstasy. A dozen thrusts, maybe more. And then they all stilled and calm silence wrapped around them like a cocoon.

Gina lay on top of Magus, her ear pressed to his powerful chest, the sound of his racing heartbeat filling her ear.

The goddess smiled. Her work here was almost done. Only two tasks were left.

She couldn't take the spirit away but she could now contain it. Magus and Cyr would no longer suffer.

She cupped her hands in front of her chest, palms facing up, and closed her eyes. Slowly, she pulled the energy released by the lovers to her. Love was the most powerful force, and this love was more potent than most. She had to draw it in gradually to keep control over it. As she gathered it, she molded it into two brilliant spheres. They hovered over her cupped hands, crackling and hissing, twin vessels fortified by a force that even Wrath could not destroy.

"Be happy." She gently blew the spheres toward the resting men and watched as the glowing orbs drifted on the current toward their targets and suddenly plunged into their bodies.

Now it was time for Gina's gift. She formed another sphere, this one from her energy, and filled it with her breath.

"Be blessed." The goddess blew the sphere toward Gina. It drifted toward her then sank into her chest, filling her with divine breath.

The mortal was now immortal.

Chapter Fourteen

🔊

The next morning, she discovered there was a message on her cell phone. From *him*, her ex-boss.

Shit.

Gina stood in the bathroom, alone, the shower running, mirrors coated with steam. She raised her hand, ready to wipe the fog away, but she stopped herself. She didn't need to see her reflection to know the truth.

Her grandmother had been right. She had been looking for an excuse to leave everything behind. She'd run away from her life, her problems. From him.

It was strange, the tricks a person's mind could play on itself. She'd told herself all along that she'd come here for her grandmother, that her grandmother needed her desperately. The fact was her grandmother hadn't needed anyone.

Quite the opposite, she had needed her grandmother. Or more precisely, she'd needed the comfort she found here, in the quiet, simple life she had once enjoyed in this very house, with the woman who loved her so well, so selflessly.

"Gina? We're heading out to work. We'll be back after six. Don't cook."

Magus. Such a sweet man. Cyr too. So opposite the dark spirit they harbored in their souls. Ironically, they looked to her as their salvation. In reality, it was the other way around.

They had no clue, but they had saved her.

She had accused them of keeping secrets, but it was the other way around. She'd been keeping secrets from them.

Silence. Sweet, glorious peace.

156

Magus gave Cyr a shock-filled glance and raced to the end of the driveway, leapt into the air, shouting at the top of his lungs, then sprinted back, tears streaming down his cheeks.

"Is it gone?" Just as overwhelmed as Magus, Cyr caught one of his arms and shook it.

"I don't know." Magus dropped to his knees, more emotional than Cyr had ever seen him before. "At this point, I don't really care. All I know is it's just…silent. Sweet Jesus, it's a fucking miracle."

"It's never been this quiet." Pulling Magus to his feet, Cyr staggered under the weight of his own emotion.

"It's the blessing. The goddess wasn't lying. Our suffering is over. It must be."

They wrapped their arms around each other and sobbed, letting tears of relief and joy flow freely, like wild rushing water bursting through a dam. Centuries of agony were now behind them, and they could finally face life like every other human on earth, with only his own demons to whisper dark demands in his mind. Even more importantly, Cyr now didn't have to fear losing the man he loved so dearly to the darkness he despised.

Sniffling, Magus pulled out of the embrace first, swiping at his red, swollen eyes. "We have to show her how much she means to us."

"We will. I have an idea."

They exchanged a watery smile.

"I know what you're thinking," Magus dragged his arm over his face again. "Tonight, we'll give her a night to remember."

"Exactly."

* * * * *

A box arrived at a little after three in the afternoon. It was delivered by some guy in a blue shirt, driving an unmarked white delivery van.

Deciding it was probably something totally ordinary, like her grandmother's medical supplies, Gina thanked the delivery man, signed the paperwork and carried the box to the couch. But then she noticed the name on the address label.

Hers.

Huh. She'd done a little online shopping for supplies, but everything she'd ordered had arrived already. Puzzled, she ran into the kitchen and returned with a knife, sliced through the packing tape and unfolded the box top.

Inside were several more boxes, all gift wrapped.

Presents? From whom? Her grandmother? Cyr and Magus? Or *him*?

Please, don't let it be.

She tore into the first one and found a pair of the hottest boots she had ever seen. Fetish wear. Definitely not from her grandma. In the second box, she discovered a gorgeous dress, again, fetish wear. In the third, an absolutely stunning pair of white and black diamond earrings. In the fourth, a matching bracelet. And in the fifth, a plain white card imprinted with the words, *Be prepared to meet your Masters at six o'clock this evening.*

Her Masters. Masters with a capital M. She'd read it right.

Cyr and Magus.

The rest of the day passed with a blur. She ate lunch while watching reruns of *Rock of Love* and *Scream Queens*. She worked on her resume and returned her ex-boss's phone call—that was the only part of the day that wasn't pleasant. After a snack and shower, she was full into the ritual of preparing herself to meet her Masters. Plucked, shaved, primped, curled.

By the time her grandmother's cuckoo clock chimed six, she was ready, dressed in her new outfit, jittery with adrenaline, and looking the best she had in weeks. Whatever her guys had planned for her, she was prepared.

A sleek black car pulled up the driveway at exactly six. At the door, she waited, expecting either one or both of the guys to come get her. They didn't. Instead, the driver, a man in a black uniform, approached the house.

He greeted her with a professional, "Madam, Misters Placett and Lambard have asked me to pick you up."

"Thank you." She headed out to the car, a nice Mercedes, a comfortable, luxurious car that rode so smoothly she couldn't tell if it was rolling on the road or hovering above it. For the first ten minutes or so, she watched the world rush by as the car carried her down several roads then onto the freeway. On and on the car drove, changing from one freeway to another. She grew tired of watching out the window so she turned on the small television in the car. She watched the news, then, curious to see how far they'd traveled, she looked outside. After checking the clock to see how long she'd been riding, she read a sign indicating an upcoming exit.

How odd. It seemed like they were driving in a circle.

"Excuse me, driver." She leaned forward as she addressed him. "Where are we going?"

"I apologize. We had to take a detour due to some road construction. It's taking us out of our way a little."

"A little? We're nearly back where we started."

"I'm sorry."

Feeling a little uneasy, Gina shut off the television and watched the road signs. They were still headed back toward home. "Could you please tell me our destination?"

"Mr. Lambard asked I not tell you."

"I'll pay you."

The driver's cool, professional mien softened a tiny bit. "I'm sorry."

"If you were genuinely sorry, you'd at least give me a hint." Even though she was suspicious, she didn't feel like she was in danger. She grew ever more convinced Cyr and Magus were up to something as the vehicle turned down the main road, leading back toward her grandmother's house. When they pulled back up in the driveway, she gave the driver a beaming smile. "Thank you so very much for the pleasant drive."

"You're very welcome." The driver excited the car, opened her door for her, and once she was up on the porch he returned to his place behind the wheel.

Absolutely bewildered, she watched the car roll back down the driveway before heading into the house.

She was greeted at the door by Cyr. He was dressed in a charcoal-colored suit that fit him perfectly. He looked amazing and she couldn't help grinning. "What are you two up to, sending me on a joyride for over an hour?"

He gave her a sweet kiss. His eyes twinkled as he looked down at her. "You'll see soon enough." His gaze wandered down her body. "You look amazing."

"Thanks to you two. How could I not? Everything you gave me is absolutely amazing."

He motioned her forward. "You've given us so many precious gifts, it was the least we could do."

"It was totally unnecessary." She didn't go further, explaining how much more they'd done for her. Now wasn't the time. She discovered a dining table set for one. Magus was standing behind the chair, his hands resting on the back. Like Cyr, he was dressed in a suit, black instead of deep gray, and like Cyr, he looked incredible.

He smiled as she entered and pulled the chair back. "Gina, first we would like to serve you dinner, and then we have a surprise."

"More surprises?" Her shoulder brushed against his arm when she stepped up to the chair, and a little buzz of sensual awareness shot through her body. She sat, thanking him over her shoulder. Meanwhile, Cyr disappeared into the kitchen. "This is so nice. But aren't you going to eat too?"

"Sure."

Cyr entered before she could respond, carrying a single-covered plate. He set it before her, and the two men sat on either side of her.

How odd. Where were their plates?

She stared down at the silver cover, polished to a brilliant gleam. Then, after giving each man a questioning glance, which was answered with a nod, she lifted the cover. "Uh...oh!"

That wasn't food.

Sitting in the center of an empty plate was a small jewelry box, robin's egg blue with the words Tiffany & Company printed on the top, a white satin ribbon tied around it.

She clapped a shaking hand over her mouth. "What is this? Magus? Cyr?"

Cyr gave the plate a little nudge. "Open it and you'll find out."

Now her hands were shaking even worse, and her throat had completely closed up. Her eyes were burning, tears gathering so quickly she had to blink constantly. She fumbled with the bow but instead of untying it, she made a knot. "I can't. My hands. Eyes. You guys."

"I'll help." Magus plucked the box from her trembling hands, dexterous fingers unknotting the ribbon and lifting the blue box top. Inside was nestled a black velvet ring box.

"Ohmygod," she whispered, not sure how she felt about what she was seeing. It was too soon to be talking about marriage— much too soon—but she couldn't shake the feeling they were about to propose.

Magus flipped the hinged top.

She slapped her hands over her mouth.

It was a ring. A gorgeous ring. Heart-stoppingly beautiful.

A large cushion cut sapphire sat at the center, its setting resembling a crown. The inverted v's forming the basket of the setting were encrusted with sparkling diamonds. More diamonds were set in the band.

That had to be the world's most amazing engagement ring.

"I don't know what to say," she said through her fingers.

"How about you just tell us what you're thinking." Cyr handed her the box. Somehow, she managed to take it without dropping it.

She ran a fingertip over the top of the stone. "I've never seen anything like it." She studied it but didn't take it out of the box, couldn't take it out of the box.

"We had it sized. I borrowed one of the rings I found in your jewelry box."

She placed the box on the plate, next to the blue Tiffany's box. "Again, I don't know what to say. It's so...soon."

Cyr sighed. "I told Magus you'd have a problem with this ring."

Magus' expression showed no hint of regret or worry. "It was too beautiful to pass up. I had to buy it for you."

She looked at the ring again. "It is lovely, the prettiest piece of jewelry I have ever seen. It's...beyond words." She pressed her fingers to her lips. "I am falling in love with you. My feelings are getting deeper every day. But I'm not ready to make that kind of commitment yet. I mean...marriage is a big step. I'm so sorry."

"Would it make you feel better if I said it wasn't an engagement ring?" Magus pulled the ring from the box and held it toward her, the bottom of the band resting on the pad of his thumb, his forefinger flat on the face of the sapphire. "I had it sized for your middle finger." As if to prove it, he took her right hand in his and slipped the ring on. It eased over her knuckle. "Perfect fit."

She couldn't help staring at it. There couldn't be a more amazing ring on earth. It felt heavy on her finger. Weighty, but good, not too heavy. "It must have cost a lot. I shouldn't—"

"Please," Magus said. "Money is one thing we have plenty of. It's nice to spend it on someone so special."

Once again, Gina was speechless. After what had happened with her former boss, she had decided never to accept gifts from a man, but it was obvious these two were so happy to give this gift, she worried she would devastate them if she didn't accept it.

Cuing into her indecision, Cyr said, "We're not trying to pressure you, and we're not expecting anything from you in return. No strings attached. It's a gift."

She traced the band with her fingertip. "It's not my birthday or a holiday. What're we celebrating?"

"Our redemption," Magus stated matter-of-factly.

"Redemption?"

"The dark spirit is silent," Magus said, blinking, tearing. "When we left this morning, it didn't speak. It didn't even whisper. We don't know if it's still inside us or not. As long as it remains silent, we don't care. It doesn't matter. All that matters is it's over. Because of you. We haven't known such peace in so long."

"Really?"

"It was you. You did this for us."

"How? I didn't *do* anything."

Cyr scooped up her hands and kissed each fingertip. It was the sweetest gesture, performed by the sweetest man she had ever known. "Oh yes you did. You opened yourself to us. Body, heart and soul. You shared the most precious gift anyone can give another."

"But there's something I haven't told you. A secret I've kept, even from myself until today. Until I find the courage to tell you, I don't think I can ever fully give myself to anyone."

Magus touched her elbow. "Tell us, Gina. Please."

"Trust us. Trust your Masters," Cyr said.

She looked at each one and as she met their gazes, first Magus' and then Cyr's, she recognized the pure love she found there. Selfless. Genuine. The kind of love she'd seen in only one other person's eyes.

These men she could trust with her body. That much she'd known for a very long time. But now, as they sat there with their hearts open, vulnerable and patient and waiting, she knew she could trust them with her heart too.

It was time to face the shame.

"I've been lying to myself and you. Since the beginning."

"How so?"

"I told you I'd come to help my grandma. But that was just a convenient excuse. I didn't leave my job, my home and my life as a selfless sacrifice, to help my grandmother. She didn't need my help—she had made plans for her care and was content to carry them out, before I dumped myself and all my problems on her doorstep. It started about a year ago," she stared down blindly as she recalled her past, shadowed, blurred images flashing through her mind. "He was smart and successful and I fell so hard, so fast. The only problem was, he was married, and his wife had no intention of giving him up. She hired a detective and threatened me, so I had no choice, I had to let him go." Surprisingly, her eyes weren't burning, her heart not twisting as she told the story. "But it's not easy to tell someone goodbye when you see him every day. He was my boss. I couldn't avoid him. I tried so hard to put it all behind me but it hurt. So I tried going to a dungeon, deciding I didn't need emotional entanglements. I just needed to fulfill some physical needs. I wouldn't let myself be hurt again."

"But it wasn't enough," Magus said, knowing her heart.

"No it wasn't."

"So you left," Cyr suggested, so certain he was right.

"No. I went back to him."

A muscle along Magus' jaw ticced, but that was the only sign of an emotional reaction Gina saw from him. "You loved him."

"No, I loved how he made me feel. There's a difference." She glanced down at the ring again before continuing. "But that's not the point. His wife made good on her threat. She sued me. She dragged my name through the mud and before I knew it, my picture was all over the local papers. In interviews, she paraded their kids in front of cameras and played to everyone's sympathy. She was brilliant. Her strategy worked. I lost everything. My job. Most of my friends. My retirement fund. And my dignity. That's when I left. I ran away to lick my wounds. Like a coward, while he kept his job, his friends, his family. He's the redeemed sinner. It isn't fair. After all, he manipulated me. Granted, I let him. I'm not faultless. But neither is he. Yet I carried all the shame and the blame."

"Do you want to do something about it?" Magus asked.

She knew this had to be killing him, listening to this story, but she had to tell him everything. "I don't know. Everything's quieted down. Most people have forgotten all about it. I'd be stirring things up again if I did, and for what?"

Magus pushed his hands through his hair. "How about to get back the dignity you left behind?"

"There is that." She stared into the depth of the stone. "I have my resume all ready, but I didn't have the guts to send it out."

"Do it," Cyr said.

Magus agreed with a nod. "You have to."

"But that means I'll be going back. Leaving here. Leaving…you."

Magus' nod turned into a shake. "For now, that's best."

"Are you sure? What about the spirit? Are you sure it's gone for good?"

"We'll be okay," Cyr insisted. "You can't let this go. We won't let you."

After a short stretch of tense silence, Magus added, "We'd rather say goodbye. Goodbye *for now*."

"Yes," Cyr agreed. "Goodbye for now."

Not one hundred percent sure she was doing the right thing, Gina returned the ring to the box and handed it to Magus. But he folded his hands around hers, forcing her to clutch the velvet box.

"No. Keep it. Even if you won't wear it yet, we want you to have it. We need you to take a piece of us with you."

"Maybe I should wait before sending my resume. My grandma—"

"No, your needs come first. Your grandmother will understand."

"That's just it—all I've done is put my needs first."

Cyr squeezed her hand. "No, that's not true at all. You've been very good to your grandmother since you arrived. Even if your initial reason for coming was self-serving—which I don't believe—you've done a lot of good for more than one person."

"I suppose you're right. It's only a three-hour drive. I can come back every weekend to visit her. And you, of course."

Cyr's smile was wistful. "We won't be home much once the seasons start. But hopefully we can work out our schedules. After the season's over we can take those dance lessons we talked about."

"I'd love that."

"Go, Gina," Magus urged. "Do it now. Get that resume sent out tonight."

"I've ruined your plans for tonight. I could wait—"

"No you haven't, and no you can't." Magus gave her shoulder a quick touch. "Do it now. By the time you're done, dinner will be ready. Go on." He shooed her from the table.

So she left, the ring box in her hand. She plopped on her bed, started up her computer and emailed her resume out to every company on her list. Afterward, still wearing the outfit they'd given her, she ate a scrumptious meal with Cyr and Magus.

The energy between the three of them was strange during dinner. The guys were pleasant, a little quiet. They hid their emotions well. Following dinner, they headed into the family room. Magus turned on the television and handed Gina the remote.

So they were in for a night of *The Dog Whisperer* and *Rock of Love* reruns?

Clearly, any plans for sex had been quashed. Gina wasn't going to push it though, not when she was the one who might possibly be leaving, and most likely breaking two wonderful, very giving and generous men's hearts.

That night, instead of the sex-fest Gina suspected Magus and Cyr had planned, the three of them watched a couple of funny movies, shared some laughs, some longing looks and some understanding looks before finally heading back to their respective beds for the night.

The next morning, Gina found a request for an interview in her email inbox. A phone call later and it was scheduled for the next morning.

While the guys were at work, she prepared for the interview and took a trip to the nursing home to tell her grandmother about the job hunt. The wily woman gave Gina an exuberant hug and sent her off with a hearty "Go, get 'em!"

That night was one of the most awkward evenings in her life. No doubt about it, she was falling for her two roomies. Falling in love.

Like last night, the evening before her interview was spent sharing a pleasant dinner with Cyr and Magus, some safe conversation about topics that had very little to do with the possible pending decision she would be making, and a strained good night in the hallway before they each disappeared behind closed doors.

More than anything, she longed to throw her arms around Magus' neck and press her body against his, lose herself in his strong, warm embrace. But she resisted the urge, as powerful as it was. And she ached for Cyr's touch, even the simplest stroke, but again, she held back, she didn't reach for him.

Hanging thick in the air was uncomfortable tension, the sort that made her shift nervously and toy with a thread unraveling from the hem of her top as she stood in the hallway wishing them a good night. They'd all agreed that they would sleep separately until she left. It would make it easier to say goodbye. It was so hard though. Just being in the next room. How would she leave the house? The city? The state?

She knew Cyr and Magus were feeling just like she was, she could read the signs in their eyes, faces, bodies. Awful, gut-twisting longing. But it would be only a matter of time — whether it was the first or the tenth interview, sooner or later they would have to say goodbye. It seemed they were all determined not to make it harder than it already was.

The next day, the interview went better than expected. If her prospective new boss — a very respected corporate attorney — had any notion of who she was, he didn't let on. She was sent home with a thank you and a promise to let her know his decision by the end of the week. The new hire would be expected to start in two weeks.

During the drive home, she tried to mentally prepare herself for the challenge of both waiting for the phone call that might send her back into the world from which she'd retreated, and the equally daunting test of living with two men she adored but had to more or less pretend she didn't. Since that night in the backyard, when they'd shared her, she'd felt this strong, compelling pull toward them. Never had it been like that with another lover, not even the man for whom she'd risked her career and future. She thought about Magus and

Cyr constantly, even while in the middle of that interview. And when they were near, she felt tingly, jittery, as if little shocks of electricity were zapping along every nerve in her body, regardless of the strain, or perhaps a little because of it.

It couldn't be just because they were beyond her reach, because she was about to walk out of their lives. No.

She loved them. Both. She loved them like she'd never loved another human being before. So much that she would do anything to make them happy. Absolutely anything.

Including taking a job that she didn't want and leaving them, because although she knew they didn't want her to leave, they needed her to be ready to move on. That meant she had to face her past.

She would be lucky to survive the next few days without going absolutely insane.

Chapter Fifteen

ဏ

Their Gina was leaving them, and Magus was falling apart. Still, despite the agony, he wouldn't let himself stop her. It took every ounce of his self-control to keep from dragging her against him, kissing her until she collapsed, and then telling her she would not leave him. He would protect her.

She was his. Theirs. Lover. Friend. Partner. Salvation. Their precious gift.

Which was why he had to be strong. It was ironic that as hard as his will had been tested by Wrath, it was being challenged even more by Gina.

She had to face her demons or they would eat at her soul and there were many things he could live with but that wasn't one of them.

She was leaving tomorrow. He wouldn't stop her. Cyr wouldn't either.

They loved her too much to do anything but gently push her to go.

Cyr scrubbed his face with his hands, the temptation to cry out with frustration so fierce he had to swallow hard several times to keep the sound trapped in his chest. This wasn't how it was supposed to end. It wasn't how he'd imagined it would be all those years as he'd fought the dark spirit to hold onto the tiny shred of his soul he had left.

Gina wasn't supposed to save them and then just walk away.

That didn't mean he didn't understand why she needed to go back to the life she'd left behind. He understood completely. He just couldn't comprehend why the goddess would send someone so special into their lives if she wasn't meant to be with them forever.

Trust in divine providence had gotten them this far. Did that mean he should just stand by and let fate move?

Time was running out. He'd loaded the last of Gina's things into the trunk of her car. She was inside, saying her final farewell to Magus. He'd stood outside to give them some time, knowing how hard this was for Magus. But he couldn't wait any longer.

He pushed through the front door and followed the sound of their voices into the family room. Magus was standing no more than a foot away from Gina, his arms crossed over his chest, his face etched with lines of strain and frustration. Both Magus and Gina turned to look his way as he entered the room.

"Well, I guess that's it," Gina said nervously, her hands gliding up and down her blue-jean-clad thighs. They were trembling a little. Cyr could see, even from a distance. Her eyes were watery, deep shadows staining the delicate skin beneath them. She lifted her arms, offering him an embrace. He accepted, drawing her against him. His nose filled with her sweet scent as her body molded to his. "I am going to miss you two very much."

"We're going to miss you too."

She tipped her head back to look at him, and his gaze immediately fell to her plump lips, quivering slightly. If only he could kiss her now.

No, you can't.

He pushed a stray lock of hair out of her face and cupped her chin. "For now, this is best. Who knows what might happen later, right?"

She visibly swallowed and nodded.

"We'll keep in touch. The season's starting for both of us in the next few weeks. I'm sure Magus explained that, right?"

At her nod, he continued, "We'll be on the road a lot. Neither of us would be home much. There's no reason you shouldn't go."

"No, you're right." A fat tear slipped from the corner of her eye. "But that doesn't make it any easier."

He thumbed it away. "Doing what's best is usually difficult."

She gave a nervous little chuckle. "You can say that again." Once again, she dropped her head and tightened her hold. "You'd just better not forget me for some groupie."

He could tell she wasn't joking, although the tone of her voice suggested she was trying to pass it off as a tease.

"Never." He pressed his hand to the side of her head, holding it against his chest. "We won't ever forget you." When he felt her hold on him soften, he released her. For a fraction of a second, he thought he might kiss her. The impulse flared through him hot and hard. But he didn't.

He regretted it the minute she walked out of the house.

Magus blew out a heavy breath after her car rolled down the drive. "Damn, that hurt."

"Yeah." Cyr dragged his hand across his burning eyes.

Their gazes met and they threw themselves into a consoling embrace, kissing each other tenderly, sharing soothing strokes and whispered words of encouragement.

"We'll see her again."

"We haven't lost her forever."

"It's just for now."

"We have to think of Gina."

For eons, Cyr had thought he'd been in hell. That was nothing compared to this torment.

* * * * *

If Gina had been told last August, after she'd said goodbye to Magus and Cyr, that her then-new job would bring her right back to their doorstep a mere nine excruciatingly lonely months later, she would have laughed. And cried. In fact, when she'd heard about the opening at McMillin, Crouch and Barnaby LLP's other office—which just happened to be less than ten miles from her grandma's house—she had done just that. And then she practically groveled for the transfer.

Thankfully, she got it, although things were touch and go there for a while. She hadn't been the first person under consideration, and she was newer to the company than her employers' partner's first choice, but she had performed well in her current position and her boss, James Crouch, had pulled a few strings and pushed through the transfer. One of those rare bosses, the kind who genuinely cared about his employees' families, he became her champion once he found out about her grandmother, still living in the assisted-living facility and as feisty as ever.

She started her new job, as assistant to Mr. Dave McMillin, a week from Monday, which gave her over a week to settle back into her grandma's house and spend some quality time with the three most important people in the world—her grandmother, Magus and Cyr. The best part—despite keeping her promise, calling Magus and Cyr every night and visiting them the two times they were home when she was in town—they had no clue. She'd kept it a secret. She couldn't wait to tell them.

Her heart not just thumping but pounding like a sledgehammer against her breastbone, she turned her car into the driveway. She toyed with her sapphire ring after she shifted it into park and stared at the house through a curtain of tears.

What a glorious sight. The crabapple tree in the front yard was in full bloom and the porch was circled in pink and white double tulips. The grass was a thick carpet of brilliant green.

The sky a crisp blue. And as she stepped from the car, the air was filled with the scent of earth and spring and sunshine.

Despite all those wonderful sights and smells, the one that made her happiest was seeing two familiar figures at the front door.

She didn't walk. She didn't even run. She sprinted toward them and threw herself into their open arms. Oh how absolutely amazing to be held by Cyr and Magus again! To sink into their embrace.

"What's wrong?" Magus' voice was deep with worry.

She smiled up into his eyes. "Absolutely nothing's wrong. Come see." Ignoring the flurry of questions they asked, she took Magus's hand in her right, Cyr's in her left, and led them back down the walkway to the car. Then she pushed the button on her key ring to unlatch the trunk and lifted. "I'm not just visiting. I'm staying."

"You're...?" Cyr stammered.

"What about your job?" Magus looked both happy and concerned.

"I got a promotion. And my new position just happens to be in an office about twenty minutes away." She yanked one of her smaller bags out of the trunk. Magus pulled it out of her hands before she could set it on the driveway. "Of course, if you don't want a roomie—"

Thunk went the bag.

Swoop went Magus' arms. And down came his head.

The rest of her sentence was cut off by a kiss. A hard, possessive one that told her there was no need to speak another word. A kiss that made her legs go softer than overcooked spaghetti and turned her brain to goo.

Now this was a homecoming!

Before she had a chance to catch her breath, Cyr had her off her feet and was hauling her into the house. Magus followed, his face flushed a deep scarlet—and not because the bags he was carrying were heavy. He slammed the front door closed behind him, after dropping the suitcases at his feet.

"What about the rest of my luggage?" Gina joked. In truth, she couldn't care less.

Cyr grunted as he claimed her mouth again. His tongue pushed past her lips, filling her mouth with his sweet flavor. A few seconds later, his mouth was replaced by Magus'. Hands skimmed up and down her clothed body, caressed, kneaded, explored. Each touch sparked a blaze until every inch of her skin was burning and she was gasping for air. Blindly, she reached for them, grabbing at their clothes and searching for skin. She shoved her hands under Cyr's t-shirt. Smooth, warm, satiny.

Cyr shoved her jeans down over her hips. Once they were to her knees, she kicked her feet out of them. Down came her underpants, and — thank God! — a hand immediately found her center. Two fingers slid inside her thrumming pussy. She sagged against Magus, letting his body and arms support her.

"Ohhhh. I've been waiting so long for this."

"And you've been waiting even longer for something else." Magus cradled her in his arms and carried her toward the basement stairs.

Bewildered, she asked, "Where are we going?" Surely there was no reason for them to go down to that dusty, musty basement now. It was full of old furniture, books that hadn't been read in decades and her grandmother's enormous collection of Tupperware, housed in a custom-built wood shelving unit. And as far as comfort went, the hard cement floor and glaring-white painted brick walls didn't provide much of a homey atmosphere.

Cyr grinned wolfishly. "We made a few improvements while you were gone. We hope you don't mind."

"Ahhh." Intrigued, she twisted a curl of Magus' hair as he carried her down the steps. He'd let it grow since she left, and she was loving it.

She was loving something else too — the update the guys had given the basement.

Gone was the old crusty furniture.

Gone was the wood unit piled with plastic containers.

Gone were the shelves and boxes of books.

Gone were the white brick walls and green painted cement floor.

In their place — a wood floor, polished to a gleam. Walls painted a deep golden taupe color. Black plush carpet that looked as soft as fur. And lots of bondage gear.

Only one word came to her mind. "Wow."

"We put everything in storage," Cyr explained, as if she might be heartbroken by the loss of her grandmother's things.

While Magus set her on her feet, she took in their new dungeon. "That's fine. If you'd told me what you were up to, I would've just told you to throw that stuff away. There wasn't anything worth keeping down here."

"What do you think?" Magus opened a huge armoire, displaying the contents. "It's all brand new, never been used."

She wanted to believe that was because they'd been waiting for her. "It's amazing."

Magus took her hand and led her toward a piece that looked like a platform with head and leg restraints attached to it. "I picked this one out for you, thinking you like to be on your back, shackled, powerless and under your Master's complete control."

He knew her so well.

"On your knees." There was a fire blazing in Magus' eyes as he bent over the platform. He gave Cyr a look, which resulted in Cyr heading for the armoire full of toys. Then he returned those smoldering eyes of his to her and watched her take her submissive position.

She closed her eyes, even though she wanted nothing more than to see his face. In the darkness, she reached for that place inside, her secret world of pleasure and escape. She heard Magus and Cyr moving around room, the clank of metal and thunk of wood. Breathless, she waited, expecting them to secure her arms, maybe tie them to her ankles. Tie a blindfold over her eyes or a gag over her mouth. Push her onto all fours or strap her to the platform. But they didn't.

Silence.

Then a fingertip ran up her spine, soft as a feather, and her muscles tightened, skin puckered. She fought a shiver.

This was going to be delicious.

Something touched her nipple and it instantly hardened.

"Push those tits out for me." That was Cyr, and ohhh did he ever have an amazing *Master* voice. Smooth, silky.

"Yes, Master." She did exactly as she was told, arching her back to force her breasts forward. She was rewarded by a soft flick of a whip. The short tail bit her skin and a rush of heat flickered through her system.

"Is this what you want?" This time it was Magus.

"Yes, oh yes."

"Can you serve two Masters?"

"Yes."

"Don't make a hasty decision, Gina." Cyr was right next to her now, practically whispering in her ear. "We're not like any Masters you've served before."

She knew that was true, and they hadn't played before.

"We don't play bondage *games*," Magus said. "It's all very real. We expect complete submission. No limits."

She was slightly intimidated by his words, but at the same time thrilled. She trusted them. After what they'd done — practically shoving her out the door so she'd go back to work, instead of letting an embarrassing past keep her in hiding — she had no doubt they would think of her pleasure and safety first.

"Yes, Master. No limits."

"You will serve us at all times, not only in this room," Cyr stated.

"Yes, Master. I will serve you both at all times. Two Masters. Your every wish and need." A little quiver of excitement raced up her spine.

"There is one other condition. Open your eyes," Magus commanded.

She opened them, finding Magus standing before her, completely unclothed, his legs braced apart, thick arms resting at his sides.

"You will have that ring resized. For your ring finger. The left one. You will promise me right here, right now, that you belong to us. To Cyr and me. For the rest of your life. So that we can serve you for the rest of our lives."

"And do we know how long that might be?" She had to admit, she'd wondered how she—fully mortal—might share a relationship with men who would never age, never die.

"As far as we know, you'll live as long as we do. At least, that's how the goddess explained it so long ago."

"Then we'll be together...forever?" Instantly, her eyes were filled with tears. "Are you sure you can live with me for that long?"

"We know we couldn't live without you another minute," Magus confessed.

She wanted to leap to her feet and throw herself into his arms, but she remained exactly where she was. "In that case, I'll get the ring resized today."

"Very good." Magus' expression softened and genuine joy glittered in his eyes. "Let us begin. It'll take a long, long time for us to give back all the love and joy you've given to us. But we are more than willing to start today, right now."

"I love you," Gina said to both of them.

"We will love you forever," Cyr cupped the back of her head and kissed her. Passionately, emotion plain in every touch of his lips, stroke of his tongue. She poured everything she had into the kiss in return. What had she done to deserve such a wonderful gift? Two gorgeous, kind, sensual, patient and strong lovers, to make every one of her fantasies come true?

When he finally broke the kiss, she was giddy, dizzy and most definitely ready to submit to them in all ways. Magus and Cyr both helped her into the equipment, and within minutes she lay on her back, her neck secured to the platform, both arms chained up over her head, and legs lifted toward her chest. Her pussy and ass were open, clenching, achingly empty and already burning. Her whole body was tight, nerves twitching from the adrenaline already pumping through her system.

She belonged to her Masters. Mind, body and soul. For with them, she had found love, the kind that would last an eternity. The kind that made her a better woman, granddaughter, lover and submissive.

And she had taken back her dignity, by facing her past, and kneeling at the feet of the men who taught her the most precious lesson of all—the true meaning of sacrifice.

* * * * *

The goddess watched, the deep furrows lining her face fading then disappearing, and once again she appeared as she truly was, not as the old woman she had pretended to be all these years. Bent, arthritic fingers straightened. Wispy white hair thickened, lengthened, until it was a mass of golden curls reaching to the small of her back. The weak muscles and delicate bones strengthened.

She couldn't stay this way for long, there was still a lot of work to do, but it felt good to be free from the frailties of mortal age for a few precious moments.

Cyr and Magus had been redeemed. The love they shared with Gina had provided the vessel that now contained the dark spirit they shared. They would suffer no more, and the three would share an eternity of blessings — the love and happiness they all deserved.

Two down, twelve to go. Who should be next to receive their reward?

Epilogue

ත

Harder. Deeper. More! the dark spirit within Troi demanded.

Nearly crippled by his need, Troi cupped his hand around the back of a man's head and pulled, claiming his lips. Their tongues stabbed, stroked, twined and battled, the spirit's deep voice resonating in his head with every thump of his heart. *More. Moremoremore!*

A stranger. Again. Two. Three. They would slake the spirit's hunger, but for how long?

Hands, four pairs, glided over Troi's unclothed body, caressing, exploring. In response, his nerves tingled, skin sizzled. He released the man he had been kissing, drawing up heavy lids to find his handsome face flushed, delicious lips kiss-swollen. This one was prettier than Troi normally liked, with fine, well-balanced features and a perfectly formed body. Smooth, freshly shaven skin stretched taut over lean muscle. A dancer's body. Graceful.

Troi's gaze dropped to the man's thick cock, ruddy and plump, the tip glistening with pre-cum. His mouth watered, yet instead of tasting the man like he wanted, the dark spirit commanded him to push the man's head down, forcing him onto his back.

Troi dropped onto all fours, the tip of his engorged rod pressing against the mouth he had only moments before tasted. He met Amun's dark gaze and thrust his hips forward.

Such was the curse they shared. The spirit of lust would never allow Troi or his lover Amun to give pleasure, only take. And take. And take. From each other and from anyone willing to serve them. Within hours of release, the monster would wake and demand more. Their life, their hell, was a cycle of brief satisfaction followed by selfish, endless fucking.

Like now. Two women and two men were caressing Troi, kissing him. While he fucked the dancer's mouth, another man's cock begged entrance to his anus. One woman's tits bounced before his eyes as she knelt before him, legs straddling the other woman's head. Nearby, Amun knelt, head thrown back, fists clutching handfuls of hair, as two women took turns sucking his cock. All around them, bodies twisted and twined together, woven by outstretched arms and bent legs. The air was thick with the smell of sex, and the moans and cries of desire punctuated the softer sounds of heavy breathing and whimpers of need.

How Troi ached to kiss those beautiful breasts before him, to suckle the tight nipples, the color of carnations, drawing hard on them until the woman before him shook and trembled with release. Or plunge his fingers into the other's sweet, shaven pussy. Her lips glittered with her honey. He could practically taste her, just by inhaling deeply. But the monster denied him.

His anus burned as a thick cock slipped inside. As if he shared Troi's pleasure, Amun leveled his head, his gaze snapping to Troi's. They shared a smile of satisfaction, even as the spirit growled, delighted by the hot desire rippling through their bodies. Fingers curled into the flesh of Troi's ass, pulling his cheeks apart. Someone else dragged sharp fingernails down his back, producing a wave of searing pleasure-pain. He let his heavy eyelids fall closed.

Moremoremore!

A set of teeth pierced the skin of his shoulder.

Moremoremore!

On all fours, he curled his fingers into the dancer's silky hair and slammed his hips forward and back. His cock sliding down the dancer's throat with each forward thrust. More pain. More pleasure. More heat.

182

"Yes," Troi murmured, his voice echoing the monster's utterings.

"Yes," Amun repeated, his voice heavy with carnal hunger.

Beneath Troi, the dancer moaned, throat tightening around his invading cock. Behind him, the man fucking his ass surged deeper, burying his thick shaft to the hilt.

"Fuck me hard," Troi demanded. In the next breath, he found a set of female lips, soft and sweet, pressed against his. He ravaged her delicious mouth, tongue assaulting hers in a lust-driven battle.

Intoxicating. She tasted of sex and man and woman.

Moremoremore!

The door creaked open. Footsteps approached. More hands. More mouths. More cocks and pussies and tits. Sounds of skin slapping skin. Moans and cries of ecstasy. The air grew ripe with the smell of sex. Desperate need hummed along every nerve in Troi's body. Muscles trembled. The dancer's mouth was replaced by a woman's tight, wet pussy.

Faster, he drove into her, fingers curled into fists on either side of her shoulders. His blood pounded through his veins, heart slamming against his breastbone. Close. He was close. The spirit's growls of pleasure grew louder, drowning out the pleasant murmurs and moans of the lovers around him, taking away what little satisfaction he truly enjoyed in the act.

Warm skin pressed against his back, silky smooth. Soft puffs of air caressed his shoulder and neck. His ear. Teeth rasped his earlobe. He shuddered. More heat blazed through his body. The monster's growls grew louder still.

Mechanically, he thrust in and out of the woman's hungry pussy. Pleasure, he took, and yet it was empty, carnal. Unfulfilling. Deep within, tension coiled through him. Once again, he exchanged a look with Amun. This time Amun's eyes were filled with desperation and despair.

Only a few more seconds. Release was a mere handful of thrusts away.

"Just a little more," he said to Amun.

He was hot. So hot. Closer to orgasm, even more importantly to glorious peace. And so he squeezed his eyes closed and took, took, took. For himself and for Amun. His cock gliding in and out of a stranger's body, her soft, slick canal rippling around him, the smell of her skin wafting over his nose.

Around him, the sounds of decadent pleasure grew louder, as if the individuals worked together as one, their release drawing closer. One thrust, two, three and he was there, breathless and shaking, at the pinnacle. A flare of heat exploded deep inside him, a keening cry shattered the quiet. His voice. A second cry echoed through the room. Amun's. In his head, the monster screeched and then grew silent as the first burst of seed raced up the length of his cock and spilled into the condom sheathing his cock.

Relief.

Peace.

So beautiful.

He drew in a deep breath, sighed and kissed the woman's sweat-dampened cheek.

Tranquil.

Still.

Silence.

If only it would last.

He glanced around the dungeon, meeting the understanding looks of Amun, Delius and Rane, scattered around the room, slaking the beast within them as best they could. Even from a distance, he could tell Amun was struggling to hold on to the tiny sliver of humanity he still possessed. They were losing the battle, both of them. Rane and

Delius weren't much better off. None of them could go on like this for much longer.

As he pulled away from the woman, he sent up a silent prayer, *Goddess, please deliver us all.*

Also by Tawny Taylor

ຄ

Wet and Wilde
Wrath's Embrace

Print Books:
Animal Urges
Behind Closed Doors
Body and Soul
Captured by Twilight
Ellora's Cavemen: Tales From the Temple IV (*anthology*)
Immortal Secrets
Master of Secret Desires
Naughty Nights
Private Games
Risque Ruby (*anthology*)
Tempting Fate
The Twelve Quickies of Christmas-Volume 2 (*anthology*)
Veiled Pleasures *with Samanth Winston*
Wet and Wilde

About the Author

ഔ

Nothing exciting happens in Tawny Taylor's life, unless you count giving the cat a flea dip—a cat can make some fascinating sounds when immersed chin-deep in insecticide—or chasing after a houseful of upchucking kids during flu season. She doesn't travel the world or employ a staff of personal servants. She's not even built like a runway model. She's just your run-of-the-mill, pleasantly plump Detroit suburban mom and wife.

That's why she writes, for the sheer joy of it. She doesn't need to escape, mind you. Despite being run-of-the-mill, her life is wonderful. She just likes to add some...zip.

Her heroines might resemble herself, or her next door neighbor (sorry Sue), but they are sure to be memorable (she hopes!). And her heroes—inspired by movie stars, her favorite television actors or her husband—are fully capable of delivering one hot happily-ever-after after another. Combined, the characters and plots she weaves bring countless hours of enjoyment to Tawny...and she hopes to readers too!

In the end, that's all the matters to Tawny, bringing a little bit of zip to someone else's life.

Tawny welcomes comments from readers. You can find her website and email address on her author bio page at www.ellorascave.com.

Tell Us What You Think

We appreciate hearing reader opinions about our books. You can email us at Comments@EllorasCave.com.

Why an electronic book?

We live in the Information Age — an exciting time in the history of human civilization, in which technology rules supreme and continues to progress in leaps and bounds every minute of every day. For a multitude of reasons, more and more avid literary fans are opting to purchase e-books instead of paper books. The question from those not yet initiated into the world of electronic reading is simply: *Why?*

1. *Price.* An electronic title at Ellora's Cave Publishing and Cerridwen Press runs anywhere from 40% to 75% less than the cover price of the exact same title in paperback format. Why? Basic mathematics and cost. It is less expensive to publish an e-book (no paper and printing, no warehousing and shipping) than it is to publish a paperback, so the savings are passed along to the consumer.

2. *Space.* Running out of room in your house for your books? That is one worry you will never have with electronic books. For a low one-time cost, you can purchase a handheld device specifically designed for e-reading. Many e-readers have large, convenient screens for viewing. Better yet, hundreds of titles can be stored within your new library — on a single microchip. There are a variety of e-readers from different manufacturers. You can also read e-books on your PC or laptop computer. (Please note that Ellora's Cave does not endorse any specific brands.

You can check our websites at www.ellorascave.com or www.cerridwenpress.com for information we make available to new consumers.)

3. *Mobility.* Because your new e-library consists of only a microchip within a small, easily transportable e-reader, your entire cache of books can be taken with you wherever you go.

4. *Personal Viewing Preferences.* Are the words you are currently reading too small? Too large? Too... ANNOYING? Paperback books cannot be modified according to personal preferences, but e-books can.

5. *Instant Gratification.* Is it the middle of the night and all the bookstores near you are closed? Are you tired of waiting days, sometimes weeks, for bookstores to ship the novels you bought? Ellora's Cave Publishing sells instantaneous downloads twenty-four hours a day, seven days a week, every day of the year. Our webstore is never closed. Our e-book delivery system is 100% automated, meaning your order is filled as soon as you pay for it.

Those are a few of the top reasons why electronic books are replacing paperbacks for many avid readers.

As always, Ellora's Cave and Cerridwen Press welcome your questions and comments. We invite you to email us at Comments@ellorascave.com or write to us directly at Ellora's Cave Publishing Inc., 1056 Home Avenue, Akron, OH 44310-3502.

COMING TO A BOOKSTORE NEAR YOU!

ELLORA'S CAVE

Bestselling Authors Tour

UPDATES AVAILABLE AT
WWW.ELLORASCAVE.COM

ELLORA'S CAVE
Romanticon

Annual convention
for women who
refuse to behave

COLUMBUS DAY WEEKEND

www.JasmineJade.com/Romanticon
For additional info contact: conventions@ellorascave.com

Discover for yourself why readers can't get enough of the multiple award-winning publisher Ellora's Cave.

Whether you prefer e-books or paperbacks, be sure to visit EC on the web at www.ellorascave.com

for an erotic reading experience that will leave you breathless.

LaVergne, TN USA
01 September 2010
195341LV00007B/3/P